D0631626

# THE ART OF MENDING

# Elizabeth Berg

# THE ART
# OF MENDING

## *A Novel*

RANDOM HOUSE ✳ NEW YORK

RANDOM HOUSE and colophon are registered trademarks of Random House, Inc.

Library of Congress Cataloging-in-Publication Data
Berg, Elizabeth.
    The art of mending: a novel / Elizabeth Berg.
    p. cm.
    ISBN 1-4000-6159-8
    1. Brothers and sisters—Fiction. 2. Repression (Psychology)—Fiction. 3. Mother and child—Fiction. 4. Family reunions—Fiction. 5. Forgiveness—Fiction. I. Title.
    PS3552.E6996A88 2004
    813'.54—dc22    2003066726

Printed in the United States of America
Random House website address: www.atrandom.com
9 8 7 6 5 4 3 2 1
First Edition

Book design by Pei Loi Koay

*For those who find forgiveness*

*by way of the truth*

*and for those who find the truth*

*by way of forgiveness*

Out beyond ideas of wrongdoing and rightdoing
There is a field. I'll meet you there.

—RUMI


Anyone's childhood can be an act of disablement if
rehearsed and replayed and squinted at in a certain light.

—CAROL SHIELDS, FROM *UNLESS*


The foxes were having their pups. . . . If a stranger
appeared near the pens, if anything too startling or
disruptive occurred, they might decide to kill them.
Nobody knew whether they did this out of blind irritation,
or out of roused and terrified maternal feeling.

—ALICE MUNRO, FROM *LIVES OF GIRLS AND WOMEN*

ACKNOWLEDGMENTS

Kate Medina has believed in me unequivocally since she first read me, and she makes no secret of it. I make no secret of this: I love her, and my gratitude to her is boundless. And I think that this time, she just needs to have the whole page to herself.

# THE ART OF MENDING

It is a photograph of a staircase that I took with my Brownie camera over forty years ago. On the newel post hang three jackets. At the bottom is mine, a turquoise corduroy, with deep pockets in which I used to hide Kraft caramels—I ate them every morning on my walk to school. Over my jacket is my brother Steve's: denim, with a fleece lining. And over that, my mother's stylish brown tweed car coat, an apricot-colored scarf spilling out of the pocket. Late-afternoon sun is streaming in through the window beside the stairs, illuminating the coats as well as three paper bags of groceries resting on the floor. I remember we'd been to Red Owl with our mother, and Steve and I had been given our own carts to select items from our own lists. That's why I took the picture: I was proud of the grown-up work we'd done. Nearly out of frame are the rounded tips of shoes. Someone sitting on the staircase, waiting for us to see her.

# 1

THIS IS THE MINNESOTA STATE FAIR I REMEMBER MOST:

It was 1960, a Saturday morning when I was eleven years old, and I was the first one up. I had brought my mayonnaise jar stuffed with dollar bills and coins into the living room, spilled the money out onto the carpet, and then stepped over it to turn the television on to a low volume. I was going to watch *The Three Stooges* while I sorted my fortune.

I had just finished counting when my father came into the room. He was wearing a pair of trousers and a T-shirt and his battered old leather slippers speckled with paint the color of my bedroom walls. His blond crew cut was damp; you could see the glistening of water in it, making him look anointed, and he smelled of a citrusy aftershave. He was headed for the kitchen, where he would make coffee and bacon. This was his Saturday routine: He'd take a cup of coffee up to my mother in bed, prepared the way she liked it, with an eighth of a cup of cream and three level teaspoons of sugar. Then she would come down in one of her silk robes and make pancakes to go with the bacon.

I always hoped she would wear her peach-colored robe. It was my favorite, for its generous yardage and elaborate ruffled trim. Seeing what my mother wore was always interesting to me, whether it was the three-quarter-sleeve blouses she wore with the collars up, or the full skirts, tightly belted, or the pastel-colored cashmere sweater sets, or one of her many bathing suits, works of art designed to showcase her spectacular figure. Those suits came complete with cunning little skirts and jackets to wear over them, and broad-brimmed sun hats trimmed with fabric bands in coordinating colors. Before she was married, my mother worked for several years for an upscale department store, parading beautiful clothes before rich men's wives. She inspired more sales than any other model before or after her; everyone wanted to look like her, though of course no one did. Think Grace Kelly with red hair and green eyes—that was my mother. But it wasn't just her model's training that made it so interesting to see what she wore, it was a quality inside herself. Charisma, my father said, but it seemed to me to be more than that. Other people had charisma. No one had what my mother did.

She had a large collection of jewelry, too; sometimes she allowed me to take one necklace at a time over to her bed, where I would lay it out and turn it this way and that, making it shine hard in the sunlight. "Are these real diamonds?" I once asked, and she said, "Why have them if they're not?"

That Saturday morning, my father saw me sitting on the floor and came over to survey my neat stack of dollar bills, my coins piled high. "How much have you got there?" he asked.

"Forty-seven dollars and eighty-three cents." I kept my smile tight to hold back my pride and stuck all my fingers between all my toes for the low pull of pleasure.

My father whistled between his teeth in a falling-bomb way I greatly admired and could not emulate despite hours of practice. He took his glasses off to polish them on the bottom of his T-shirt, then held them up for inspection: still dirty—he never managed to get them completely clear. "How'd you get that much?" He resettled his glasses on his face, pushing them up snug against his nose, a gesture I associated so strongly with him that I reflexively took issue with others doing it.

I said I'd been saving for a long time. I told him about the groceries I'd carried in for Mrs. Riley, "Mrs. Five Operations," my mother called her, for her incessant replaying of the laminectomies she'd endured. I'd pulled weeds for Muriel and Helen Lockerby, the two wild-haired old-lady sisters who lived around the corner. I'd babysat for little Rachel Thompson every Thursday after school while her mother went to run errands, and I'd occasionally walked their dog, an arthritic old German shepherd named Heintz, who seemed to me to grimace every time he lifted his leg. I'd made pot holders and sold them around the neighborhood—once, a man who answered the door in his bathrobe had bought my entire week's inventory, which made him in my eyes equally wonderful and weird. Also, though I did not tell my father this, I'd recently found a ten-dollar bill on the street, and I'd made no effort whatsoever to find the owner.

My father told me to wait for just a minute and disappeared. I sat immobile, my high spirits on hold, because I thought he was going to consult with my mother about how much I'd have to share with my eight-year-old sister, Caroline, who had saved little, and my seven-year-old brother, Steve, who had saved nothing at all. But that's not what happened. Instead, my father reappeared, holding his wallet. He took out a twenty-dollar bill and handed it to me. Mutely, I put it on the bottom of my pile, so no one would see. But I found out later that each of us kids had received the same gift.

I still remember what I brought home from the fair that day: a lantern that glowed Gatsby green in the dark, which I intended to take under the covers with me to read by; a bag of Tom Thumb doughnuts so redolent with the scent of cinnamon sugar it nearly levitated me; a poster of a brown mare and her foal, lying in a field full of daisies. The rest of the money I'd spent on rides and on chances to win something big on the midway. Over and over I tried, and over and over the carnies at the tacky wooden booths smiled and said, "Sorry. Want to try again?" They knew what I'd say. From the time I was quite small, I had about me a certain air of heedless determination.

When my funds were gone, I went to the blanket my parents had spread out near the edge of the fairgrounds. This was our meeting place, our refueling station—our family went to the fair once a year and stayed there all day. We kept a cooler filled with drinks and sandwiches and fruit, deli containers of various salads, Oreos and Chips Ahoy!—all this though we knew we would be gorging on fair food. There were also pillows and Band-Aids, suntan lotion and insect repellent, aspirin and a couple of Ace bandages. My parents took turns manning the station, sitting in a lawn chair and amusing themselves in their own way—my mother flipping through fashion magazines or crocheting, my father doing crossword puzzles or reading one of the historical tomes he so enjoyed. He tried often to interest us kids in history, saying it was invaluable for putting things into perspective. "You think something's really great?" he'd say. "A long time ago, there was something just as good or better. You think something's really bad? Look in the past—you'll find something worse. Think something can never happen again? Wrong! History repeats itself— *that's* what you can be sure of." But we, like most children, did not resonate much to things beyond the day at hand. History had nothing to do with us.

My father also liked people-watching—he could sit for hours and

stare at all the fairgoers who passed by him and feel perfectly entertained. He just got a charge out of people, their frailties and foolish-
ness as much as their more admirable characteristics. I remember
once lying in bed and overhearing an argument between my parents.
This was a rare thing; they almost never crossed each other. But that
night my mother was yelling: "Is *everything just fine* with you, then?"
After a moment, I heard him say simply, Yes, everything was. An ac-
cusatory silence followed. I rose up on one arm and leaned toward
my parents' bedroom wall. I heard the ticking of my bedside clock;
the movement of night air in the trees outside my window; then, finally, the even, comical sounds of my father snoring. I lay back down
and fingered the buttons on my nightgown, and contemplated the
disturbing possibility that my parents were not perfect.

On that day at the fair when I came back to the blanket, my
mother was off with my brother and my sister was with a new neighbor her own age whom we'd brought along in the desperate hope that
Caroline and she would become friends. My father was alone. I sat on
the blanket beside his chair, and he gave my shoulder a little squeeze.
Then he moved out of the chair to sit beside me. He looked at me for
a long moment, then asked, "How are you doing, Laura?"

I held my hands out, palms up. "I spent it all."

"Yes," he said. "But I meant, how are you doing in general? Is
there . . . well, how's life treating you?"

I smiled. I thought he might be kidding. Sometimes he would ask
me about politics in the same false and jocular way. "How about that
Eisenhower?" he would say. And I would shrug and say, "*I* don't
know." But his expression now was serious; he asked me again how
I was, so I said, "Good, I guess." Then, feeling this was not enough,
I described my excitement at finding out I'd be getting the teacher I
wanted that year at school: Mrs. Lindemeyer, who was old as the hills,
and an easy grader.

My father nodded. "So you're okay, then, are you? You're happy?" The question was odd to me—I didn't ever really think about whether or not I was happy—but I said yes. It seemed he was looking for something he couldn't name and I couldn't decipher, and the closest I could come to satisfying us both was for me to say I was fine; I was "happy." He returned to his chair, and we sat in uneasy silence until the others returned.

My brother, his mouth rimmed with red from a candy apple he'd just eaten, had spent all his money too. My sister had spent none. I remember being astounded at this; angry, too, that Caroline would be left with so much when I now had nothing. "How can you have fun if you don't even spend any money?" I asked her.

A pleated caramel-apple wrapper skittered by, and she captured it beneath her shoe. "I had fun."

I snorted. "How?"

She looked up at me, an irritating calmness in her eyes. "I watched." The new neighbor, Linda Carmichael, confirmed this: While Linda rose high up in the sky on the Ferris wheel, Caroline stood watching and waving from below.

"That's retarded," I said. I could tell Linda agreed with me, and I remember thinking that she and Caroline would never be friends; here was yet another opportunity Caroline had lost.

"You mind your own business, Laura," my mother said quietly. That's what she said when I told Caroline she was stupid not to eat the treats that were handed out at various classroom celebrations, too. Every time there was a party at school, Caroline ate nothing. No candy corn at Halloween, no message hearts on Valentine's Day, no red- and green-sprinkled spritz cookies at Christmas, no garishly decorated cupcakes brought in because someone in class was having a birthday. Instead, anything she ever got she tented with paper towels and then carefully carried home on the school bus. As soon as she walked in the door, she presented it to my mother and my mother ate it.

I never understood this about Caroline. Now I do. It's all clear now: the times Caroline, as a small child, lay in the hall outside the bathroom door while my mother bathed. The presents she later bought for her with babysitting money: barrettes, scarves, lipsticks. Paperback books and velvet roses. "Brownnoser!" I once whispered after she'd given my mother a bottle of dime-store perfume. Caroline ignored me; she sat at the kitchen table where I was doing homework and began pulling books and papers out of her schoolbag. She was in sixth grade then, and I in eighth. "Brownnoser!" I said again, out loud.

"Laura," my mother said, and I returned to my homework. There was a tiny smile on Caroline's face, and I kicked her under the table. She did not kick me back; rather, she moved away to another chair and straightened with pinched-nose efficiency a stack of notebook paper that did not need straightening. She cocked her head slightly to the left and the right as she did it. I hated it. I glared at her between narrowed lids; I believed I could feel heat coming from my eyeballs. All this was to no avail; Caroline looked at her schoolwork only.

Then came a gift I remember particularly well, something given to my mother by Caroline the Christmas she was sixteen. It was the last gift opened that year, and it was a framed photograph, an 8-by-10. My mother stared at it briefly, murmured a low thanks, and started to put the picture back in the box.

"What is it?" I said. "Let me see!" I snatched it away. The picture was of Caroline wearing one of my mother's slinky evening gowns, her hand on her hip. Caroline's auburn hair, the same color as my mother's, was styled in a twist like the one my mother always wore. Her makeup was heavily applied in a style exactly my mother's own, and she stared unsmilingly into the camera. It was chilling, the look on Caroline's face: the flat eyes, the hard line of mouth, the *remove*. I had never seen such a look. "What is this supposed to be?" I asked.

My brother took the photo from me and looked at it. He burst into laughter, the goofy adolescent-boy kind, and Caroline grabbed the picture from him and threw it onto the floor. "It isn't for you," she said. She turned to stare at my mother, who did not look back at her, and then left the room.

"Caroline!" my father called after her. "Come back here!" But she did not return. My father rose, as though to go after her. Then he saw the picture, and he sat back down.

This I understand now, too—as well as what my father meant that long-ago day at the fair, when what he was really asking was if I knew.

# 2

I WAS THE ONE WHO WAS SUPPOSED TO GET MARRIED first. I was the oldest, I was the one who was boy crazy, and I was the one with overly strong domestic leanings. I preferred putting a tray of Snickerdoodles in the oven to things like playing Capture the Flag or roller-skating or going swimming. I did like making joke phone calls, and lying in the grass staring up at the sky held a certain dreamy appeal. Occasionally I would play a board game, or jacks, or venture alone into the out-of-doors, where I would often be pleasantly surprised by what I found. But my mind was mainly on the world of homemaking and fake flesh; the biggest reward of a nature walk was that I could come back with a bouquet for the cardboard kitchen cupboard of my "house," a generous corner of the basement I had appropriated at age five and had no intention of ever giving up. I had a rug remnant for my living room, and two folding chairs placed side by side and covered by a chenille bedspread served as a sofa. I had a photo of a television from the Sears catalog taped to the wall. The photo was absurdly small, of course, but my imagination was not. I had a good-sized cardboard box lying on its side to serve as a coffee table, and my mother's discarded magazines were fanned out there in imitation of the way she arranged her own. Nearby, dolls lay sleeping in cribs or sitting in perpetual alertness in the rickety high chair.

Years later, I told all this to a therapist, a Dr. Madeline Marrone, who asked me to "start our work" by telling her about my favorite place as a child. I saw that therapist on a dare by my chronically unhappy college roommate, who insisted she saw signs of a deep unacknowledged depression in me, but who actually, I came to believe, merely wanted a companion in her own dark trench. The therapist suggested that a serious disorder in my family made me seek such specific comfort in my own small "home." But I didn't think so. I thought I just liked caregiving and eating cookies warm from the oven. I declined to make another appointment, and I changed roommates.

My relatives still make fun of me for my love of things domestic, especially my Aunt Fran, who, whenever we visit, always tells me she's saved her ironing and mending for me. Actually, I wouldn't mind doing it. I like ironing. It's the physical equivalent of staring into middle space. I think it waters the mind, if you know what I mean. As for mending, I think it's good to take the time to fix something rather than throw it away. It's an antidote to wastefulness and to the need for immediate gratification. You get to see a whole process through, beginning to end, nothing abstract about it. You'll always notice the fabric scar, of course, but there's an art to mending: If you're careful, the repair can actually add to the beauty of the thing, because it is testimony to its worth.

My sister, Caroline, got married early, at barely twenty years old.

She'd stayed the weird one, the one we all thought would never find anyone. But she married another architecture student she met when she was a freshman at the University of Minnesota. She's been married for thirty-one years now and lives in a house an hour away from my parents. Her daughter, Eva, is grown and gone, a public relations consultant living in Los Angeles.

My brother, Steve, got married before me, too. He's gotten married a lot. He's on number four, a sweet woman called Tessa—I hope this one will last. No kids for him. His children are his boat and his airplane, the new car he buys every year, and the bar that he owns, called Pud's. It's located on Rush Street in Chicago, and according to him it's the hippest place in the city.

But I waited a long time to get married. I was forty when I finally fell in love with a man who was a widower. He'd been married exactly one week when his wife died. Car accident—she'd gone out for butterscotch topping for the sundaes they were going to have after they finished wallpapering their bathroom. He didn't date for five years after her death, and he didn't think about marrying again until fifteen years after that, when he met me. Her name was Kate. She was a lovely black-haired woman who taught nursery school and wrote exquisite poetry. I know Pete is devoted to me, but I also know that a corner of his soul is reserved for her. I don't mind. She deserves it. And so does he.

Pete comes from a big Italian family. His parents, Rosa and Subby (for Sabastiano) Bartone, visit us at least twice a year, making the voyage by RV from their retirement village in Arizona to our ramshackle house in North Dakota. I can honestly say I'm always sorry when they leave. I put flowers in their room before they come; they leave homemade pasta sauces in my freezer before they go.

Pete and I have a daily routine, which started when we were dating. Every night, sometime after dinner, we tell each other about an incident that occurred that day, and then we share a memory from the past. It began as a corny but extremely effective way for us to get to know each other. Now it's part of the way we stayed grounded and entwined. My neighbor and best friend, Maggie, says you have to have a lot of sex in your marriage because it works like glue. So does this.

Many of the memories Pete has shared have had to do with his parents. He's told me about vacations to Alaska and about smaller moments spent sitting at the kitchen table. One of my favorite memories has to do with a time he sat with his three sisters and his little brother, eating biscotti dipped in cocoa for an afternoon snack while they watched his mother make dinner. She spoke softly in Italian to the red sauce she simmered in the Dutch oven, to the gigantic meat-balls she rolled, to the gold-colored rosemary-scented focaccia she put on a TV tray out on the front porch to cool. She went out to the garden and made a bowl of her apron, and Pete filled it with lettuce and peppers and white-freckled tomatoes.

He's told me about his father sitting on the edge of the bathtub, playing his banjo and singing songs from the old country for his wife, who soaked in her milk bath. And about the time his father was instructed by Rosa to harshly discipline Pete and his brother, Danny, for the crime of stealing a pair of their neighbor's gargantuan underpants off her clothesline and using it to wax their bicycles. Subby took the boys into his bedroom, shut the door, and whispered to them to howl while he struck the mattress repeatedly with his belt. They were a little too convincing; when they all filed back into the kitchen, Rosa planted her fists on her hips and said, "You think you make a fool of me?"

My memories don't often focus on my parents, and if they do the stories are not like my husband's. Much of our food, for example, came from cans, and our dinners were mostly silent. Eating was not something to be celebrated. It was done because it had to be, rather like cleaning out your ears. You ate, you bused your dishes, and then, as quickly as possible, you went back to the more interesting and rewarding parts of your life. It took many years for me to understand what people meant when they described the joy of a good olive oil, the perfect balance that comes with mixing goat cheese with fig compote and black-olive tapenade.

My family did not go on vacations together. Our summers were lazy and unstructured; we kids were left to come up with our own entertainment, and I loved it. There'd been one summer when we were sent to camp, each of us to a different one, but that must have been seen as a failure, at least in my parents' eyes—we never went again. I'd been glad about that. My camp had a predictable dearth of domestics and what was, in my opinion, an overabundance of physical challenges. In addition, I'd been afraid of Cynthia Mayfield, a hugely overweight girl who constantly threatened to beat me up for no reason I could discern; and I'd been equally afraid, though for another reason, of the raven-haired Jinxie Benson, who sat cross-legged on her bunk every Sunday night making lists of who was cool and who was not—and why. These lists were circulated among the campers and were eagerly—if anxiously—read and taken to heart, even by the counselors, who confiscated and denounced them but also had been known to sit at their table in the back corner of the cafeteria poring over their own personality reviews. I'd been suspicious of the Chapel Under the Pines, thinking it fostered idolatry. And what was one to *do* with Eyes of God?

So the stories I told Pete focused less on my parents and more on me and my siblings. There was the time I'd told Caroline I had the ability to turn myself into another person, someone called Kathy, who looked like me but was in fact someone entirely different, and she believed me. "What do you think of Laura?" I'd asked, and then, later, when I'd "turned back" into Laura, I'd punished Caroline for the negative things she'd said about me. "How did you know?" Caroline had asked, massaging her punched arm, and I'd said, "Kathy told me."

I told Pete about the time I made my little brother sit in the corner of my basement house for a couple of hours in order to be my husband. "What do I *do*, though?" he'd asked, and I'd said, "Nothing. You're at work." While he sat idly scratching his ankle, humming tunelessly, practicing belches, and then, finally, lightly dozing, I busied myself. I rocked babies, vacuumed (using a discarded canister model I'd found by someone's garbage, a five-star discovery), and made tissue paper carnations for a window box I planned on making out of the next shoe box that came along. I chatted on my plastic telephone. Finally, I made a chocolate cake in my Easy-Bake oven and awakened my husband to share it with me. "It's *raw*," he complained, which earned him immediate expulsion from the basement. Not that he'd minded.

It often came to me, telling these stories to Pete, that there'd been a terrible cruelty in me as a child, but then I suppose all children have such moments. A friend of mine told me about the matter-of-fact notation she used to put at the top of her diary page almost every evening: J.C. This was not a religious ritual but acknowledgment of the fact that once again her brother, Jason, had cried that day. She'd never tried to find out why; she hated crybabies. Once when she and her brother were in their forties and having a drink somewhere, laughing and talking about their growing-up times, she apologized in an offhand way for never having made inquiries as to the nature of his despair. She expected him to wonder what she was talking about; instead, he stopped smiling and said, "Well. It's about time."

Pete and I had children right away, and though I feared the results of the amnios, and then of the births, both our boy, Anthony, and our girl, Hannah, couldn't be healthier. They're fourteen and twelve now, respectively, and Pete and I are beginning to realize we've gotten our freedom back. We haven't had a babysitter in two years; and I'm finally able to do my work in a way that allows me to focus for long hours at a time.

I make my living as a quilt artist, and for the most part the work I do is commissioned. I charge a hundred and fifty dollars a square foot, not without guilt. But I have whole days when I stand at my design board moving pieces of fabric around, and I don't sew a stitch. Then something clicks, and I hit the machine. The money I charge pays for the thinking time too; I explain this to my clients. And people do pay it, willingly—I have more clients than I can handle. The wait for a finished quilt is four to six months, but people don't seem to mind that, either. I think there is a longing for things that reflect a certain kind of slowness; perhaps the pendulum is beginning its inevitable swing back. I'll be glad if it does—I'm computer phobic and one of the few people left in America who don't have e-mail. A friend once told me she didn't want e-mail because she doesn't understand how it works. Well, I said, you don't know how a mixer works, either, but you use that. True, she said, and added that it was pretty depressing to realize the only equipment she *did* understand was what she used for hanging out the wash, and even then she didn't get the spring-type clothespins, only the little people ones.

I don't even have a cell phone, though I am just about ready to get one of those, mostly due to Anthony's constant reminders that soon he'll be driving and really has to have one in case of roadway emergencies. I can envision these "emergencies": *Dude! I've got the car; want me to come and pick you up?*

Pete keeps saying that if I continue to do this well with my quilting, he's going to quit his job and live off me. I tell him, Go ahead, but I don't think he ever will. He owns the hardware store in the center of town, and he loves being there. It's how I met him. I'd come to town for a quilting convention, and I needed some wooden dowels. For me, it was love at first sight—I asked him out to dinner that night, and by the time we had dessert I was fantasizing our fiftieth-anniversary celebration. Pete's the kind of guy who doesn't mind spending fifteen minutes helping old ladies pick out just the right plate hanger from his carefully organized bank of plastic drawers. Oftentimes those ladies come back the next day with a basket of muffins for him and his staff. He'll give them a kiss on the cheek and they'll make embarrassed little Aunt Bee clucking sounds and smile, all but waving the hankies they store up their sleeves, in a mix of plea-sure and distress. I met Pete at a time when I was ready for a truly nice guy, out from under the wildly erroneous assumptions that danger-ous men are fun and inconsistent men are interesting. You can have your pouty-mouthed bad boys; I'll take the guy most people would fault with being overly sentimental. "That's because you're *old*," Hannah said, when I told her recently about the qualities I prize most in a man, and she was probably right. That, and I'm pretty sentimen-tal myself.

TODAY I NEEDED TO GO to the fabric store to select the yardage I wanted to use for the border of a quilt I was making with Japanese overtones. It was for a woman who believed she'd lived many times before and that one of those past lives was as a geisha. It's funny how people reveal themselves in the quilts they commission. One client had a bitter divorce but she wanted me to use her wedding dress to make a quilt that honored marriage. A truck driver commissioned a wildly feminine floral design to sleep under when he was on the road. A woman alienated from both her children had saved every item of clothing they'd ever worn as babies and toddlers, and she had me use them along with items of her own clothing to create a pattern of interlocking circles. She wept when I delivered the quilt to her and then hid it away in a box she'd bought especially for it.

After I came home from the store, I needed to pack for our annual drive to Minnesota the next day. It was state fair time again. Everyone in my family went, every end of August. Our annual family get-togethers, like most people's, were a mix of great fun and misery. They were what I did precisely one year after I'd said I'd never do them again. And each time, I could hardly wait to get there.

# 3

IT WAS UNUSUALLY QUIET AT FABRIC WORLD. I LINGERED at the shelves of blues for longer than I might have ordinarily, knowing I wouldn't have to wait a long time to get my selection cut. Two store employees, Joanne and Ellen, stood leaning against the cutting table chatting and laughing quietly, their arms crossed. I'd been coming to Fabric World for years—Hannah actually took her first steps here—and until recently you never saw the employees relaxed like this. They'd always been told that if there were no customers, they should straighten bolts of fabric, cut up remnants for quilt packs, even dust shelves. Now there was a new manager, a flamboyantly gay man named Gregory, who had made everyone's life better. He designed wedding dresses in addition to working at the store, and he gossiped viciously about all his clients, much to the guilty enjoyment of everyone around. He answered the store phone saying, "Fabric World, what *now?*" I still didn't quite understand how he was hired, never mind made manager; the owners of the store were rumored to be quite conservative. I thought it was because Gregory couldn't help being charming, even when he was insulting you. And people trusted his taste—they bought anything he told them to.

"This is beautiful," Joanne said, when I brought the cobalt-blue fabric I finally settled on over to the table to be measured and cut. There were black cranes printed on it, some standing on one leg, some flying, their wings thrillingly outstretched.

"It's for a border," I told her. "I need a yard and a half."

She began cutting and we stopped talking, both of us listening, I think, to the sound of the scissors. For those of us enamored of the world of textiles, this sound is a little symphony. It conjures an image of a head bent over a machine, the feel of fabric slipping through fingers, a small light focused on a field of intimate labor.

I saw Gregory on the other side of the store, stopping to straighten some of the colorful bolts in the juvenile section. When he noticed me, he came over to the cutting table. "Help," he said. "I've dreamed about seed pearls for the last three nights."

*Seed pearls!* I thought. Maybe a few scattered across this quilt I was making. And binding made of a fabric that suggested water—some wavy, indistinct lines of blue on white.

"What are you working on?" he asked.

"Something sort of Japanese, this time. A lot of circles mixed with squares."

"Sounds divine. *Anything* but a wedding dress sounds divine. I want to make my niece some very cool pants, but instead I have to labor on a dress for a whale. I mean, why doesn't she just wrap up in a lace-patterned shower curtain and call it a day?"

"Great attitude."

"The truth hurts. Hey, have you got time for a cup of coffee? Come in the back with me and I'll show you some samples of things I just ordered."

I looked at my watch. "Can't. I've got to go home and pack—we're going on vacation tomorrow. I'll take you up on it when I get back, though."

"Ta-ta," he said, walking away and waving over his shoulder. And then, to Joanne and Ellen, "Which one of you wants to give me a full body massage? No fighting, *please*."

After I got in the car, I took the fabric I'd bought out of the bag and stretched it across my lap so I could sneak looks at it on the way home. Before I'd taken the first cut, I'd already transformed it a thousand times.

WE ATE PASTA FOR DINNER, with some puttanesca sauce that Pete's mother, Rosa, had made and I'd defrosted in the microwave. I was amazed at how the flavor held; no one could cook like Rosa did. "Have you packed yet?" I asked Anthony.

He nodded, his mouth full.

"Yes?"

He nodded again, less emphatically, then shrugged. "Almost."

"What does that mean?" Pete asked.

"It means I know everything I want to bring. I just have to put it in the suitcase."

"Right after dinner," I said. "We're leaving early."

"I *know*." He rolled his eyes. Beneath the table, I suspected, his knee was bobbing up and down.

"How about you, Hannah?" I asked. "Did you lay out what you want to take?"

"Yes, and I can pack by myself now. I don't need you to do it."

"Well," I said. Meaning, *Yes, you do*. If I let Hannah pack by herself, she'd put in books, her Swiss Army knife, art materials—everything but what she needed most.

"Why are you such a control freak?" she asked.

I looked quickly at Pete, surprised, although he accused me of the same thing often enough. "Why must you oversee *everything*?" he once asked. We were in the family room, watching a movie we'd rented that neither of us much liked, but neither of us had the energy or inclination to turn it off. Instead, we talked over it. "I don't oversee everything!" I'd said. He'd stared at me, a half grin on his face. Then he'd said, "Okay. I just said, 'I think I'll get a snack.' You said, 'There's frozen yogurt or beer pretzels.' Am I not capable of choosing my own snack?"

"I'm only suggesting," I'd said. "I know what's around because I buy the groceries. I know what's fresh—I'm actually protecting you. I'm trying to prevent a bad snack experience."

He didn't respond to my attempt at levity. "Stop trying so hard to prevent things from happening," he'd said. "What are you so afraid of?"

"Nothing," I'd said. "Choose your own snacks from now on. Get salmonella." But the very next time he said something about wanting a snack—in the same situation, actually; we were in the family room watching a movie—I said, "There's licorice in the cupboard." And then I'd stared intently at the screen so he couldn't say, *See?*

But this was a different situation. "Hannah," I said. "I'm not trying to control anything. You just need a little help packing, that's all."

Hannah readjusted her headband, then patted the top of her head. She spent hours grooming now; in the kids' bathroom were at least seven products for her hair alone. "I'm done," she said, pushing back from the table. "I'm going to call Gracie, and then you can *help* me, 'cause I'm too *lame* to pack by *myself*." She flounced out of the kitchen, a defiant gesture that merely served to entertain the rest of us.

"Why don't you help *me*, Mom?" Anthony said. "In fact, you can pack everything for me."

"You can do it yourself."

"No fair," he said, grinning. He tipped his chair back on two legs. "Hey, Dad. I saw this car for sale? Two blocks over?"

"No."

"Just to work on. It's only fifty bucks! We could keep it—"

"No," Pete said. And then, though I knew it would only make matters worse, I said, "Anthony."

"What?"

"Chair."

He sat forward, righting the chair, muttered, "Jesus."

"What was that?" Pete asked.

"I said *Jeez*. Okay, Mr. Cleaver?"

"I heard what you said."

Anthony looked at me, shook his head. Neither of us was sympathetic to Pete's inability to tolerate any word that is or approximates a "swear," as Hannah called it. But I usually let it go—I did, after all, have my own proclivities toward extreme old-fashionedness.

"Hey, Dad."

"What."

"Would you buy me a concert ticket for the fair?"

"I suppose."

"Would you buy me two?"

"Who's the other one for?"

"I don't know. I might get lucky."

Pete started clearing the table. "Yeah, I'll buy you two concert tickets."

"All right!" Anthony stood, stretched. "I'm going to pack now. Then I think I'll stay up all night so I don't have to get up early." He pulled my apron string as he walked past, then told me, as he always did, "Hey, Mom. Your apron's untied."

I started rinsing the dishes while Pete finished clearing. "So today," he said, "this old lady comes into the store and asks me where

I keep the pliers. I tell her, and she goes back there for a really long time. Then she comes past the checkout counter with a pair of pliers sticking out of her purse. 'Excuse me,' I said. 'You going to pay for those?' And you know what she says? She says, 'Well, I wasn't planning on it.' "

I looked at him, laughed.

"I swear!"

"So who was it?"

He shrugged. "Beats me. Jeannie said she thought it might be Theresa Haggerty's mom, who's visiting her from Florida. I guess she's not quite all there."

"I guess *not*. So, did she pay?"

"Yeah, she paid. And then she tried to give me a tip."

I shook my head, smiling, and rinsed the last of the silverware, loaded the dishwasher, and set it to start a few hours later.

"So what happened to you today?" Pete asked, sitting down again at the kitchen table.

I sat opposite him. "Let's see. I got a call from a woman who wants a quilt made for each of her seven grandchildren. *And* I saw three ducklings cross the street by Save Mart. All the traffic just stopped, waiting for them to cross, and them taking their sweet, waddly time. I love it when that happens—kind of puts things in perspective."

Pete smiled. "Yeah, it does."

"And here's a memory for you," I said, "Once, at the fair, I went into the tunnel of love by myself. I was Hannah's age. Ahead of me was this couple, kissing away. And I just couldn't stand it, I wanted so much to have a boyfriend. I took my gum out my mouth and threw it at them. I wanted it to get in the girl's hair."

"Nice."

"I know."

"So what did she do?"

"I missed. It landed on the back of the guy's neck. He got really mad. He turned around with this killer look, and I yelled, 'I didn't do that! I don't know where it came from; I just saw it fly past. I didn't do it!' I'm sure he knew I was lying, but he went back to his girl-friend."

"You want me to take you in the tunnel of love this year?"

"Yes. And on the Ferris wheel. And to the pig barn. And to see the butterheads. And to the cheese curd stand, and for roasted corn and caramel apples. And pie. And Swedish coffee. And to see the tractors and the home improvement stuff. And I'll go to the technology build-ing with you if you'll come to creative arts with me. I want to see the dog shows. And the horse shows—I don't want to miss the Lipizzan-ers again."

"Go help Hannah pack," Pete said. "I'm exhausted already."

JUST BEFORE I FELL ASLEEP, the phone rang. Pete answered, then said, "Oh, hi, Caroline; here's Laura," and handed the receiver to me. He's never been one to chat on what he calls a modest instrument of torture, but you would think he might have learned to be a bit less abrupt. My sister was used to it by now, of course, but I was always having to explain to new friends that my husband was really a very nice guy, he just had no telephone etiquette.

"Were you sleeping?" Caroline asked.

"Not yet."

"You weren't . . ."

*"No."*

"Okay. Listen, I'm sorry to call this late, but I wanted to catch you before you got to Mom and Dad's. I've been . . . there's something I have to do."

"Yeah? What is it?"

"Well, I want to have us kids get together, just by ourselves—you, me, and Steve. A restaurant, maybe; we could go out for dinner or something."

"Why?" To plan Mom and Dad's anniversary? I wondered. It would be fifty-five years this September: admirable, but not something you usually make a big deal out of.

"I want to talk about some things."

"What things?" I began to get alarmed. "Is it something about your health?" Pete turned on the bedside lamp, mouthed *What's up?* I lifted my shoulders: *I don't know.*

"No, it's . . . I've just been thinking a lot, lately, about the way we were brought up, and I—well, there are some things I want to ask you and Steve, with no one else around. This will be a good time to do it. Bill's not coming this year; he's going to finish putting in our new bathroom. And Tessa won't be there either; Steve said she's got to be in Atlanta. Pete won't mind if the three of us take off for a couple of hours, will he?"

I didn't know whether to be worried or annoyed. "But . . . Caroline, just tell me, what do you want to talk about?"

"I don't want to get into it now. But I'd really like to have us all get together. Would you just help me arrange it?"

"Well, *yeah.* We'll pick a day when we're there and just do it. It's not that hard."

"I'd hoped we could pick a day now. And then maybe you could call Steve and let him know. It'll be harder for him to say no if you and I have already agreed to it. Would you please do that?"

"Fine. How about the second night we're there? The first night we'll have to hang around. But the next night we'll go out somewhere. How about Snuffy's; you want to go to Snuffy's?"

"Anywhere. Thank you, Laura. So you'll call Steve tonight?"

"It's better with Steve if you don't plan ahead. I'll just tell him. He'll come."

"Okay. I'll see you tomorrow."

I leaned over Pete to hang up the phone and lay down again. "Caroline wants to talk to me and Steve alone. I don't know what about."

"Is she upset about something?"

"No, I wouldn't say upset, exactly, but she sounds kind of . . . intense."

"Well. What else is new?"

"This felt different. She says she wants to talk about some things that happened when we were growing up. I hope she doesn't mention the time I told her about Jesus on the cross. I hope she forgot about that."

"Why, what did you say?"

"Oh, just . . . you know, I told her the story of the crucifixion. And made her cry."

Pete turned out the bedside light, settled down under the sheets, yawned. "That's not so bad."

"No, you don't understand. Religious education wasn't the goal. Making her cry was. Not that it was hard. Caroline was always oversensitive. She cried if you looked at her wrong. Literally." I moved closer to Pete, closed my eyes.

"I'm waiting," he said.

"Why do you have to be such a good listener?"

"What did you say?"

"Well, I overdramatized a bit, okay? I talked about how it hurts when you stick a pin in your hand. And then I said, 'And just imagine. They put NAILS in. They *pounded* NAILS in.' Stuff like that."

"You said that? That *is* pretty bad."

"Yeah, I know. But you did some terrible things to your brother and sisters."

"I can assure you I stayed out of the God area."

"Yeah, but when Stella was only four, you told her you turned into a werewolf at night."

"How do you know that?"

"She told me. And she also told me that you lined shoes up along the top of your door and then yelled for Danny to come quick, and when he pushed the door open all the shoes fell on him. And gave him a black eye."

Silence.

"You robbed Tina's piggy bank twice."

"All right. Good night."

"Oh. Oh! And you—"

He leaned over, kissed me. "Good *night*. We have an early morning." He turned on his side, closed his eyes, and fell asleep. It's amazing. Head on pillow, and he's out.

I lay awake, wondering what was up with Caroline. I thought of the drive ahead of us, how the kids would ignore each other for the most part but how there would also be a few fights to contend with. It was only a five-hour drive, though, and then we'd be there. The garden would be perfectly tended, the bird feeders would all be full. There would probably be sheets and upside-down shirts and pants on the clothesline; my mother was a big believer in line drying. One summer I'd tried it myself, but the romance had drowned in the inconvenience.

The food would not be memorable, of course, but the setting would be nice. We'd eat out on the back porch on a green painted table with an embroidered tablecloth, nice old flowered china, a huge vase of flowers, and the cut-glass salt-and-pepper shakers that had belonged to my grandparents—whenever I saw them, I remembered those shakers being on their Formica kitchen table. I remembered, too, my grandfather using his tongue to pop his lower dentures out of his mouth, then gulping them back in, one of the many things he did to thrill us grandchildren. For a long time, I hadn't known they were dentures, and I'd thought my grandfather was an extremely talented man. I had spent long periods of time lying on my bed trying to loosen my own bottom teeth so I too could perform this interesting feat. My mother had come into my room one day with a laundry basket and had seen me yanking away at my back molars. "What are you doing?" she'd asked. And when I'd told her I was trying to do Grandpa's trick, she'd laughed and told me his teeth were false.

"But where are his real teeth?" I'd asked.

"Gone."

"But gone where?"

"I don't know," she'd said. "Just gone."

"But—"

"Laura." She'd touched my shoulder. "Don't ask so many questions. You always ask so many questions. Don't do that. Just . . . accept things." She'd moved to my dresser to put away neatly folded stacks of underpants, talking with her back to me. "Don't ask questions and don't look back. Believe me, you'll be much more content."

I'd grown silent, trying to figure out what *that* meant. Then I'd gone back to thoughts of my grandfather's teeth.

It was strange how my memory was changing. More and more, someone would refer to something that had happened fairly recently, and I would have forgotten all about it. I misplaced my glasses, the cinnamon, the name of an actor I'd always known. An abiding comfort was that it was happening to Pete too. "Guess who was in the store today?" he'd say. And then he'd get this panicked look on his face. "It was . . . oh, you know. You know who I mean." We would stand in the kitchen, blankly staring at each other. "Oh, man," he'd say. "Hold on a minute." He'd concentrate for a while, eyebrows knit together, arms crossed, one foot tapping the floor, and then he'd throw his hands up in the air and give up. Hours later, he'd remember. Or not.

Other things, especially from times long ago, I remembered clearly. I recall, for example, every detail about a time I lay on my belly next to the stream that used to be half a block away from our house. It was a hot morning in July; I had just turned ten, and I'd wanted to go somewhere to be alone and consider my oldness—two digits! I remember the algae swaying seductively in the greenish water, the quick thrill of a school of minnows swimming past, the grit of dirt against the exposed strip of skin at the top of my yellow pedal pushers. I remember the onion-scented smell of the long grass there, and the way it imprinted a pattern of itself against your skin after you lay in it.

That same summer I buried Necco wafers in the dirt and then dug them up again and ate them, to show I was not afraid of germs. The sun had been setting gloriously when I popped the candy into my mouth; I remember the sky looked as though it were on fire. There'd been a ring of admiring neighborhood kids around me, including a six-year-old girl picking her nose rapturously with one hand and holding a Tiny Tears doll wrapped in a pink-checked blanket with the other. I wanted very much to hold that doll, but for obvious reasons I feared touching it. A twelve-year-old boy, the senior member of the impromptu gathering, had tossed a baseball from hand to hand, weighing insult versus compliment, I knew. In the end, he'd split the difference and had said, "Huh!" before he walked away.

And this memory has persisted too: my mother holding a laundry basket against her hip that day she came into my room, telling me what she believed was necessary for living a happy life.

It is my grandfather, sitting in a nubby green oversized arm-chair in his living room. The flash of the camera is captured in his eyeglasses. He is wearing his gray cardigan sweater, a plaid shirt, and some loose-fitting pants. On one side of his lap, I sit holding a lollipop and leaning back against him, smiling. On the other side is Caroline. Though my grand-father has his arms securely around both of us, she is trying to pull his arm closer still. Her fingers appear to be digging into him. She looks tense and unhappy, trying so desperately to delay his letting go that she hastens it. I remember the exact moment after that photo was taken: a sudden gust of wind lifting maroon draperies printed with exotic lime-green fronds; the smell of frying chicken in the air; my grandfather standing up to go into the kitchen "to help Grandma make the gravy"; and me pinching Caroline because I knew it was she who made him leave. I cautioned her not to tell or I would pinch her again, harder.

# 4

MY FATHER HAD SENT US AN ARTICLE FROM THE *PIONEER Press* about some things that would be at the fair this year, and Anthony was slumped in the backseat of the car, reading aloud from it. We'd been driving for three hours, and an edgy monotony had set in.

"There'll be two hundred and fourteen port-a-johns," Anthony read. "And they'll use twenty-two thousand rolls of toilet paper."

"Gross," Hannah mumbled.

"What's gross about toilet paper?" Anthony asked. "What would be gross is if there *weren't* any."

*"Eeeeuuuuwwww!"* She returned to her paperback, a story of three teenage girls who explore the Arctic by themselves.

"They'll have elk ragout," he said. "And walleye on a stick."

"That walleye's actually very good," Pete said. "I've had that. I might get it again."

"Listen to this breakfast," Anthony said. "Smoked pork chop, scrambled eggs, fried dumplings, and a kolach. I'm getting that."

"I'm eating *only* fried food," Hannah said.

"Well, you're in luck. Listen to this: They have fried ravioli, French fries, cheese curds, onion blossoms, and fried dough. And look at this: deep-fried *pickles*! Hot damn!"

I saw the color rise in Pete's face at Anthony's mild epithet, and he started to turn around but opted instead for paying attention to the road. But his eyes sought out Anthony's in the rearview mirror.

"Sorry," Anthony said quietly.

"You know, Anthony, you just don't seem to get some things," Pete said.

"I *said*, Sorry!"

"He's smiling," Hannah said. "He's not sorry."

"Hannah!" I said, at the same time that Pete said, "I can see him, Hannah."

It was thickly quiet for a moment, and then Pete said, "I guess if you can't remember to respect my rules, I can't remember to give you money for concert tickets."

"Dad, I'm sorry, okay? It just slipped out. It's not—I don't know why you get so bent out of shape about this! It's just an expression everybody uses. I don't get it, why you're always so—" He stopped, exasperated. Stared out the window. "It's *weird*," he said, under his breath.

Pete put the blinker on and moved to the right lane to pull off into a rest stop.

"Uh-oh," Hannah said. "You're gonna get it."

"Pete," I said, "don't be so—"

But he stopped the car, cut the engine, stared at me in a direct bid for support, and turned around to look at his children. "There are certain things in your life that will become very important to you," he said. "You might not be able to explain to anyone else why they're important. But you will expect the people who love you, the people who are your family, to respect those things. If any of you need to swear, do it somewhere else. It *bothers* me."

"But—don't get mad, Dad, okay?" Anthony said. "I just wish you'd tell me *why* you think it's so bad."

Pete faced forward and rubbed the back of his neck. "Just . . . don't. Okay? I tell you again, don't do it around me. *Period*." He started the engine.

"Do you want me to drive for a while?" I asked.

"I'm fine."

"I'll drive," Hannah said, and I was relieved to see Pete's small smile. I too once asked Pete why it was so terribly offensive to him when people swore. It had been many years ago; we'd only been dating a few months. We were out walking in a park, and I'd asked more or less the same question, and Pete had stopped to examine a leaf on a tree. He'd been turned away from me when he'd said, "It's just . . . it's a need I have. It doesn't matter why."

"Okay," I'd said. And I thought maybe I'd have to stop seeing him—his answer had made me really uncomfortable, and I had a habit of swearing a lot. But there'd been nothing else so tightly wound about him. Anyway, by then it was too late: I loved the planes of his face, his black hair and blue eyes, his elegant table manners, his deep voice, his love of animals and children, his otherwise easygoing manner. I loved *him*. I would forgive him this and hope he would forgive my own irritating mannerisms.

"They have sixty-five rides," Anthony said, reading again from the newspaper.

Silence.

"In 1965," he said, "Princess Kay of the Milky Way wore a formal gown made of butter wrappers."

"All *right*," Hannah said. "Just be quiet, now, I'm trying to read."

"Okay, but just one more thing. You know what else?"

She sighed. "What?"

"You know how they make those sculptures out of butter? The head of Princess Kay of the Milky Way?"

"Yeah. And her court."

"Right. Well, most of them freeze their heads. But this one princess? She melted hers down for a corn feed."

"Let me see," Hannah said.

I leaned my head against the window and tried to doze while peace reigned, but I couldn't. First I imagined that practical Princess Kay dressed in jeans and a plaid shirt and loafers, hair in a ponytail, standing over a Dutch oven in some farm kitchen, watching her likeness melt down into nothing. Then I thought of my parents, waiting for us. My mother would be wearing some new outfit she'd purchased for the occasion, and she'd meet us at the door, chatting a mile a minute. My father would be puttering in the basement, and when we arrived he would solemnly come into the kitchen to offer his muted greeting. Standing in that familiar place, I believed I would feel the usual odd mix of sensations. Some of it would have to do with the inescapable nostalgia and apprehension—even preemptive irritation— that accompanies any visit home once you've moved out. The rest would be because of something I'd always felt but could never name. My mother, smiling brightly, looking directly into your eyes before she embraced you tightly, would feel a million miles away. My father, averting his gaze before he took you into his arms, would be the one who felt close.

# 5

MY MOTHER WAS OUT CUTTING FLOWERS WHEN WE
arrived, bent over roses such a deep red color they looked
black. She turned when she heard our car doors slam and
shaded her eyes. She was wearing a white linen blouse,
black linen pants cut to just above the ankle, and red
strappy sandals. Cute. "Look who's here!" she cried, and,
removing her gardening gloves, headed toward us, arms
open wide. "You're the first ones. I'm so excited!" She
hugged Pete and me, then the kids. "You've grown!" she
told Hannah.

"You always say that," Hannah said, smiling.

"I know. But it's always true. You've become a *lovely*
young lady." She turned to Anthony. "And you! You're
gorgeous!"

Anthony laughed, embarrassed, then took his bags and
headed for the back door. "Grandpa inside?"

"Down at his workbench," my mother said. She

started to take one of the suitcases, but Pete took it from her. "Save your strength, Barbara," he told her.

As we headed indoors, we heard a car honk. It was Steve, pulling up to the curb, and then we saw Caroline's car pulling up right behind him.

"Well!" my mother said.

"Good timing," Pete said, but my mother seemed more unsettled than pleased. She smoothed down the collar of her blouse. Raised her chin. It seemed to me that there was, in these movements, a strange sense of preparation for battle. But then I decided my perspective was skewed by what Caroline had told me the night before. I waved at her and Steve and headed inside.


IT WAS ALMOST MIDNIGHT. Pete and I were lying in bed in the basement guest room, a room my parents used mainly for storage of out-of-season clothes. Beside us, in the dim light of the moon coming through the tiny, high windows, I could see our makeshift nightstand: a TV tray holding an alarm clock, a tiny lamp, a box of Kleenex, and a small porcelain dish, put there, I knew, for holding Pete's change. There was a cozy completeness to this utilitarian still life. It occurred to me that one of the values of going away was that you saw that something far less complex than what you were used to would do just fine. More and more, I looked at my house, at my life, and thought, *Why do I need all this stuff?* Maggie and I had been talking about this need to simplify, about what it might mean; she'd been feeling it, too. "It's the first step in getting ready to die," Maggie had said, in her usual no-nonsense way. "It is not!" I'd said, but I thought she was probably right.

Upstairs, I could hear the muted conversation of my parents, still up and sitting in the TV room. Soon they'd go to bed and then continue talking quietly, I knew, until they fell asleep.

I lay there, Pete beside me, and the sound of my parents' voices seemed to erase him; seemed to erase me too, at least as the middle-aged person I was. I became instead a young child, fresh from the bathtub and smelling of Ivory soap, the doll I'd chosen for the night mummy-wrapped in a receiving blanket and held in the crook of my arm. I was not responsible for anything but my own daily meanderings. The purpose of reading the newspaper was to check up on Nancy and Sluggo. Monetary decisions had to do with what kind of candy to buy with the change I had left over from going to the corner store to buy milk for my mother. My parents were my clock and my calendar; they told me where to go and when. My parents were also the arbiters of judgment, of taste, and of politics; I stepped into their values like an outfit they'd laid out for me on my bed. Later, of course, I forged my own beliefs and rebelled against nearly everything they'd taught me. But every time I came home, some large part of me surrendered itself to the past and relished the sense of being the one who was cared for, if only by a TV tray serving as a bedside table. I was in my mid-fifties, but in my parents' house I was forever made to feel uniquely safe by the late-night murmurings of the people who were in charge, leaving me free not to be. No matter what anyone said, it seemed to me that not only *can* you go home again, you are helpless not to.

I dozed lightly, then woke up again. I'd been dreaming of Caroline, or at least thinking of her in the kind of nether land that precedes sleep. She'd been remarkably quiet at dinner and seemed to be trying to catch my eye at odd times. Something was really bothering her.

I looked at the clock: 1 A.M. I leaned over Pete, gently touched the top of his head, whispered his name. "Are you sleeping?" No response except deep breathing. I got out of bed quietly and headed upstairs to the kitchen. I turned on the stove light and went over to inspect the contents of the refrigerator. Here were the things I rarely bought anymore but always wanted to eat: butter, salami, heavy cream, cheese, mayonnaise. In the cupboards were great varieties of cookies and chips. And in the bread drawer, white bread and a box of cinnamon rolls covered by thick frosting. My father had high blood pressure and cholesterol problems, but my mother disbelieved certain tenets of modern medicine. She had a particular disdain for mental health workers. When I once told her about a friend of mine who was in therapy, she'd said, "Psychiatrists. They're crazier than anyone." There'd been no humor in this remark. There'd been venom in it.

I was sitting at the kitchen table having a salami sandwich when Caroline appeared, ghostlike in this dim light. "Hi," she whispered. I waved at her, my mouth full. She opened the bread drawer, took out the package of cinnamon rolls, brought it over to the table. "I can't believe I'm eating again," she said. "It's like coming home late at night when we were in high school. Remember how hungry we always were?"

I nodded, smiling. "Yeah. Remember the time you and Steve and I were eating and he dropped that bowlful of spaghetti all over the place?"

Caroline took a huge bite of her roll, talked around it. "And he really wanted it, so he ate a bunch of it off the floor."

"Right." I finished my sandwich and went over to the cupboard to take a look around. "Want some Oreos? Oh, boy, they're double-stuffed."

She didn't answer, and when I looked over at her, I saw her face pressed into her hands. "What's wrong?" I closed the cupboard and came back to the table. "Caroline? What is it?"

She smiled sadly. "I'm sorry. I don't want to talk about it now. Not here. It was just . . . a moment."

"They're asleep," I said. Amazing how quickly we could lapse into the shorthand of sides: us versus them; kids versus parents.

"We'll talk when we go out. When Steve's here too."

I leaned back in my chair, picked up a cinnamon roll, and started unwinding it. "I was dreaming about you just before I came up here."

"Were you?"

"Yeah. You were upset."

"Well, I *am* upset."

"Well, I *know.*"

She stood, tightened the belt on her robe, and put the box of cinnamon rolls back in the drawer. "Anyway . . . I'm glad you're here. I'm glad we all are."

"Yeah. Me too."

"So . . . I'll see you in the morning." She sighed. "I'm sorry I'm such a wreck. But we'll talk, okay?"

She turned to go and I grabbed her hand. "Hey, do you want to go out now? Take a car ride?"

"I want Steve to be here too."

"Want me to wake him up?"

"No. I know you'd love to, though."

"He used to like it when I woke him up late at night."

"He's older now."

From upstairs, we heard the sound of a toilet flushing. "I'm going back to bed," Caroline said quickly. The hall light turned on, and she disappeared into the living room, where she was bedded down on the sofa.

Then the overhead kitchen light turned on and my mother was standing there, squinting against the brightness. "Is everything all right?"

"Yes, I was just hungry. I had a little snack."

"Are you the only one up? I thought I heard talking."

"Caroline was up. But she went back to sleep."

"Oh?" She looked back toward the living room, then expectantly at me.

"She was just up for a minute. You didn't miss a thing. Go back to bed."

I started for the basement steps and she said, "Are you comfortable down there? Cool enough?"

"We're fine."

"Because I've got another fan if you need it."

"We're all right."

"Maybe that little revolving one. You could put it on the night table."

*"Mom!"*

She raised her hands in surrender. Then she turned to exit the room, that old runway spin.

"Mom?"

She turned back.

"Thanks, though."

"You're welcome."

Pete awakened as I climbed back into bed. "Hi," he said sleepily, pulling me close to him. He kissed my neck, started caressing my breast.

"Don't," I whispered.

"Why?"

"It's my *parents'* house."

"And?"

"Come on. I can't do it in my parents' house."

"I can," Pete said. I kissed him quickly, then turned away from him, saying, "Go to sleep." But then, after a moment, I reached back and put my hand on his thigh, and we both stayed up awhile longer. Sometimes it embarrassed me, how happy we were. Sometimes it seemed like I was making it up.

# 6

I WAS UP EARLY, STARTING COFFEE IN THE KITCHEN, when my mother appeared. "I don't think I slept more than three hours last night," she said.

I turned, coffee measure in my hand, midair. "Why?"

She sat heavily at the table. "Your father. He said he felt dizzy last night, and then early this morning he said his arm felt numb."

"Oh, my God, it's his heart!"

"No, no, it's not. It's nothing like that. He just had a checkup. I think he slept on it wrong."

"Let me take a look at him," I said. As if I'd know anything. But I was the oldest, so I acted like I did.

"He's asleep again. I'm sure it's no emergency. Let him be."

"You're sure?" I looked toward their bedroom.

"Yes. Believe me, this is not the first time he's kept me up half the night with one complaint or another that turns out to be absolutely nothing. He's beginning to become a bit of a hypochondriac. It's hard not to, at our age, when so many of our friends . . ." She stood, took the coffee measure from me. "Anyway. I'll do this. And then let me make your breakfast. What would you like, French toast? Pancakes?"

I sat back down at the kitchen table. "Just coffee. The kids will be up soon, and then we're going right over to the fair."

"Are you all going together?" She flipped the switch for the coffee and sat down with me. Almost instantly, the satisfying aroma of brewing coffee filled the air. "Are Steve and Caroline going with you too?"

"Yes. And you and Dad are coming too, right?"

"Maybe you should go on ahead of us—he was awake so much last night. Call me in a couple of hours. I'm sure he'll be up by then, and we'll figure out a place to meet."

"Are you're really sure he's all right?"

"I'm sure. When he wakes up, he'll be in better shape than *I* am."

Caroline came into the kitchen, yawning. "Is the coffee done?"

"In a minute," my mother said.

"Yeah, but I need a cup right now. Don't you have one of those coffee interruptus things?"

"It'll be done in a minute, Caroline."

Caroline sat at the table with us. "I suppose you'll be wanting to go on the roller coaster again," she told me.

"Don't I always?"

"Aren't we too old now? It'll kill our backs."

"It didn't hurt last year," I said.

"Yeah, it did."

"Did it hurt just *you* or both of us?"

She smiled and fastened her long hair up into a twist that she anchored with a barrette she pulled from her robe pocket. "Actually, you complained for hours after we got off."

"Really?"

"Yes."

"Oh."

My mother got up to put coffee mugs on the table. "I haven't been on one of those things for thirty years. Your father used to make me go with him, but I always hated it. I kept my eyes shut and gritted my teeth the whole time."

"Wasn't your first date with Dad at the fair?" I asked. We grew up hearing stories about my parents' romance. The most interesting one had to do with the time my father was in the navy and got a letter from my mother, who at that point was his fiancée. He opened the envelope on deck on a windy day, and the letter blew out of his hand. He actually jumped into the ocean after it.

"But that's crazy!" I'd said, when I head the story. And he'd said, "Yeah, I guess it was. A lot of my shipmates said the same thing. They thought it was wrong for a man to be so much in love with a woman." He chuckled. "But I was." Then, leaning closer to me, he'd said, "I still am, too."

I'd said, "Well, that's great, Dad," but I wasn't sure I really meant it. I appreciated the outlandish sentimentality of his diving into the drink, but I thought his friends were right: To love someone that much was a dangerous thing.

The coffeemaker beeped and I got up to pour for all of us. My mother took a sip, then said, "Well, you remember that we met at the movies. And we sat together that night. But, yes, our first official date was going to the fair. We were nineteen years old, can you imagine? Your father had never paid to get into the state fair in his life. It was a matter of honor with him. So he gave me money to get in and told me where to meet him. Then he went and snuck in under the fence."

"What fence?" I asked. "I'll send the kids, save a few bucks."

"It's not there anymore," my mother said. "And shame on you."

"Shame on her?" Caroline said loudly. "*Shame* on her?"

My mother and I both looked over at her. "It's a joke," I said finally.

"No," Caroline said, "it isn't."

"Caroline," I said, sighing.

"Is it, Mom?"

My mother, flustered, started to answer when the basement door off the kitchen opened and Pete appeared. "Morning!" he said. And then, "What's wrong?"

"Nothing," we answered, all three of us together. And then, while my mother poured coffee for Pete, Caroline headed for the bathroom and I went upstairs to tell the kids to get ready.

## 7

PETE, STEVE, AND THE KIDS WERE ON THE ROLLER coaster for the second time. Caroline and I were sitting on a bench waiting for them. Caroline was right—we were too old to go on that ride. My rib cage hurt from where I'd slammed into the side of the car and Caroline's knee was bruised from the safety bar. "Tell you what," Caroline said, "let's make a deal. Let's support each other in vowing never to go on that damn ride again. If anyone asks, we stand together in our absolute refusal."

"Fine with me," I said. My back hurt too.

Caroline leaned against the bench and smiled at the sight of a mother pulling a wagon by us, two sleeping children in it. She looked at her watch. "Eleven o'clock. They conked out early, huh?"

"They've probably been here since six," I said. Seeing a pattern I liked in the leaves of the tree across the way from us, I pulled a small sketch pad out of my purse and did a rough drawing. It was the overlapping quality I liked, an edge next to an edge next to an edge.

Caroline looked over my shoulder. "What's that for?"

"I don't know. Something."

She sighed. "Always working."

I looked up at her, surprised. "I'm not always working!"

"Yeah, you are. You've always got your nose to the grindstone about something. Always."

"No, I don't!"

"Oh, don't get so upset. It's not a criticism. It's just an observation. You've always been that way. Busy, busy, busy." She tossed back her hair, now hanging in loose curls, and pushed her sunglasses up on top of her head. "It's getting cloudy. Do you smell rain?"

"No." I did, actually, but my anger made me want to disagree with her. I was thinking about what she'd said: *Busy, busy busy.* Was I? I stretched out my legs. "So what are you going to talk to me and Steve about, Caroline?"

"Not now."

"Just tell me what it's *about.*"

"I did tell you. I want to compare notes. I have a lot of bad memories, and I need to know, finally, whether . . ." She crossed her arms over herself, then crossed her legs. If she were a turtle, I thought, she'd pull her head in. But then she looked directly into my eyes. "This is what it is," she said. "I just feel like I can't get past some things until I talk this out with someone who was there when I was growing up."

I started to say something but didn't. Instead, I nodded. Sort of.

"I know," Caroline said.

"What?"

"I know you think I'm a pain in the ass."

"Oh, it's not that," I said. "I just . . . well, frankly, Caroline, I worry about you. I mean, when does it ever just get easy for you? I wonder if you need to just stop thinking so much. Feeling so much."

"I don't decide to feel what I do. It just comes. I wouldn't mind not feeling so much, believe me."

I turned toward her, attempting a tone of compassionate reason. "But . . . can't you decide what to do *with* it? Can't you—?"

"Laura, I've come to a point where I just have to know some things. That's all. I can't even work anymore. I've become obsessed with finding out what happened to me that made me so . . . well, I just feel like if I can find out some things, if I can validate them, I can finally head in a different direction. I won't feel this terrible sense of . . ." She teared up. Then, tightfisted, she stared straight ahead. When she spoke again, her voice was angry. "I don't know why I'm telling you this. I don't think you can understand what I'm talking about at all."

"Oh, come on, I—"

"No. It's not the same for you, Laura. We're so different. We always have been. I love you, but we're just . . . different." She looked down at her hands. "I've been seeing a therapist. I started a few months ago; I'm going twice a week. At first I was getting nowhere. I'd walk out of there feeling guilty that I was spending a hundred and twenty-five dollars an hour for nothing. Well, not for nothing. For trying to entertain a woman who was supposed to be helping me. But what finally happened is that I stopped goofing around and started doing some real work. It helps. Before I went, things had gotten really bad. I hadn't even been able to get out of bed on some days, I just . . ." She looked over at me. "I couldn't get out of bed."

"Why didn't you tell me?"

"I don't tell you things like that. I don't tell anybody in the family things like that! Do you? I mean, for one thing, I know when you feel bad, you don't exactly get immobilized and lie in bed all day. You'd never do that. You'd leap up and make a cobbler." She reached out to touch my hand. "I mean that in a complimentary way, okay? I really do."

She was right. I was more like Maggie, who, the last time she was sad, painted her garage and then, in a fit of good neighborliness, painted ours as well.

"I couldn't tell anybody I knew, really. So I started seeing this therapist and we got into some childhood stuff, and I remembered some things that were . . . I remembered some things that were pretty awful. And then all of a sudden I started to doubt myself. I started to think maybe I was making it up, maybe this was some sort of therapy-induced fantasy. And I need to talk to you and Steve to see if you remember any of it as well."

"But you mean . . . abuse of you?"

"Well, yes, basically. But of a very specific kind."

"Like . . . sexual?" An image of my father came to me: Best Loved Teacher, year after year, standing before a class of high school freshmen, their faces raised to him.

"No. No." She looked over at the roller coaster. "Look, we can't get into it now. We need time. And also I want to talk to you about . . . I think Bill and I are getting divorced."

"*What?*"

"Yeah." She raised her eyebrows, smiled an ironic smile. "Eeeeyup."

"Well, Caroline, you . . . I mean, you sort of add this *on*! This is a big deal! They're both big deals!"

She stood and pulled her purse higher on her shoulder. "Here come the kids."

I stood up beside her. "I hate it when you do this," I said quietly. I smiled and waved at the little group coming toward us. "I hate it when you start something and then just—"

"You're the one who pushed to talk about it. I wanted to wait until later." She smiled widely at Hannah, now beside her. "How was it?"

"Awesome! We're all going *again*! Just one more time!"

"Hey, Mom!" Anthony said. "Come with us! Please?"

I started to say no, but then agreed to go. It wasn't often that my kids asked me to do things with them anymore. I handed my purse to Caroline without asking if she'd mind holding it.

It took awhile to get through the line, but finally we all climbed on board. Once, when the front car I was riding in with Hannah hesitated at the crest of an incline, when it took that agonizing pause before starting its mad descent, I looked over and spotted Caroline sitting alone on the bench, our purses in her lap. She looked so small. I suddenly remembered our promise to each other never to go on this ride again. And then it occurred to me that I didn't forget it at all.

Caroline is sitting on her heels in the dirt, wearing her blue dress with white rickrack trim. She is about seven years old. I am standing above her taking the picture: you can see my elongated shadow on the ground beside her, my short braids bowing out from the sides of my head like broken handles. I have caught Caroline burying something, and she will not tell me what it is. I say I am taking her picture because she looks so pretty, but that is not the reason. I am taking it so I will know where to look, later, when I sneak out and dig up what she is trying to hide. She smiles shyly, her hands folded in her lap, squinting in the bright light. I never do return to the site. I am not interested enough to go back and look for anything of hers.

# 8

WE WERE FINALLY GETTING CLOSE TO THE END OF THE long line for cheese curds when a tall and massively overweight man wearing dirty jeans, a black T-shirt, and a black leather vest cut in front of us. He was entirely nonchalant, sliding in as though we were holding a place for him. He was balding but had a long stringy ponytail hanging halfway down his back and many gold hoops on one ear. He reeked of beer. I looked at the kids and started laughing. But Caroline tapped him on the shoulder. "Excuse me," she said. "You just cut in front of us."

The man turned around.

"Caroline . . ." I said.

"No! He cut in front of us!"

The man sneered, then turned away.

"Excuse me!" Caroline said again, louder, and this time Steve said quietly, "Caroline. Let it go."

She looked at Steve for a long moment, and I saw the

tension in her jaw from clenching her teeth. Then: "Fine," she said. "I'll wait for you outside." She walked away and Hannah shouted after her, "Aunt Caroline! Do you want us to get you some?"

She turned back, shook her head no, and disappeared into the crowd.

"Whoa!" Anthony muttered.

"She's just a little nervous today," I said.

"She's always like that! Seems like any little thing—"

"Enough," Pete said. "She was offended by this guy's bad manners. She's right—he shouldn't have cut in front of us."

The man turned around, belched in Pete's face, and put his back to us again. I saw Pete waver for a moment, as did I, and then we all exploded into laughter.

When we reached the counter, I ordered cheese curds for Caroline anyway. She'd eat them. I knew her.

When we came outside, we saw her sitting at a picnic table piled high with other people's litter. She was on her cell phone, frowning. She held up a hand to indicate that we should be quiet. *Busy, busy, busy,* I wanted to say to her. But when she snapped the phone shut, she said, "That was Mom. Dad's at St. Joseph's Hospital."

The image of my mother appeared, dressed in the robe she'd had on that morning, waving away my concerns about my father.

"Do we have to leave?" Hannah asked.

"Yes." I took her hand and started walking quickly. Ten minutes to get to the exit, at least. Another fifteen to walk home—that would be faster than trying to get a cab through this traffic. I'd told her it was his heart and she'd said to leave him alone. I'd known it wasn't right. I'd known it and I'd listened to her anyway.

"Is it okay to eat my cheese curds?" Hannah whispered, and I nodded a tight yes. It would take fifteen minutes to get to the hospital, if there was no traffic.

During the quick and silent walk home, I did not think of my father.

Instead, I thought of Caroline, of all the times she'd come home from school, crying. Or come in from outside, crying. The way she would moon over a book where some horse died. The way she would go to sad movies over and over. I was so tired of her theatrics, her fragility, her deliberate forays into melancholy, her complicated secrecy—not just now but always. I worked myself into a pretty nice state of anger at her, which kept me from having to think about what my father might look like right now. I had lived this long and had only seen a dead man once. He was lying on the floor of a shopping mall, right outside the entrance to Penney's. His face had been gray-blue, his mouth slightly open. There'd been a woman kneeling beside him who was attempting CPR, in vain. Her purse and shopping bags lay scattered about her; and one of her shoes had come loose off her heel. "He's gone," she'd kept saying, but then she would give him another breath and pump on his chest, counting aloud in a high voice that shook a little.

I'd thought, *This morning, he picked that shirt to put on.* I'd thought, *I wonder why he came to the mall today.* And then I'd walked away. I'd told myself that it was because it was indecent for people to make a ring around the man, gawking at him. But the truth was, I'd left because I couldn't stand looking at him and realizing people die. As soon as I turned away, I'd told myself to forget about him. And I had. I'd gone into a store three doors down and looked at bath oil, and then I'd bought some. All the way home, I'd imagined not the sudden loss of another soul on earth but rather how nice it would feel to be submerged in warm water, breathing in the scent of white gardenia. It had been so easy to erect my barricade against fear, against pain, against knowing. Now it seemed that my house had blown down. I was about to meet the wolf.

AUNT FRAN WAS SITTING IN THE WAITING ROOM of the ICU when we arrived. She was wearing light-colored pants with circles of dirt stains at the knee—clearly, she'd been working in her garden when she was called. She shared a love of gardening with my mother, but there the similarities ended. Where my mother was stunning, Aunt Fran looked . . . friendly. The same could have been said of Steve and me; it was only Caroline who inherited my mother's great beauty. I was "pleasant looking"—I'd heard that all my life—with widely spaced brown eyes and even features. I used to have a good body, but now I suffered the usual humiliations of getting older. Steve looked like an All-American boy, even at his age.

There was another and more important difference between my mother and my aunt. Where my mother was uptight, Aunt Fran was unfailingly relaxed and open. I had loved visiting her as a child. I used to ask her why she couldn't be my mother. I'd concocted a fantasy whereby she in fact *was* my real mother; she just gave me to her sister because she had too many other children. But I preferred being around Aunt Fran. She let you crawl onto her lap, she read to you with clear enthusiasm, she told jokes, she let you eat cookies between meals, she sang loudly along with the radio, she helped you build sheet tents and cardboard forts, she asked you about your life because she really wanted to know the answers.

Once, she'd been lying out in her lawn chair on a hot summer night, and her fourteen-year-old son and I were sitting in the grass on either side of her. We were drinking lemonade from aluminum tumblers with little terry-cloth wraps that kept your hand from getting too cold. We'd just finished brownies that Aunt Fran had whipped up on the spur of the moment: just like that, no problem, made from scratch, no recipe. "Tell me about the stars, Eric," Aunt Fran had said. And he had, and she'd listened to him in wonder, her eyes wide and staring upward into the darkness above her.

He had begun by saying, "Well, our sun is a star," and Aunt Fran had gotten all excited and said, "Really? Really?" I'd listened to the rest of what Eric said, and the whole time I'd had a thought flitting around my brain like a moth repeatedly bumping into the light: This is what a family really is. This. This. This.

Mostly, when you were around Aunt Fran, you enjoyed a buoyancy of spirit: There was nothing *wrong*. There had been a thickness in the atmosphere at our house, a vague and ongoing sense of something amiss. It was the kind of thing you didn't particularly notice until you were away from it. But once, when I'd asked Aunt Fran yet again if I could live with her, she sat me down for a serious talk. I was seven, but she treated me as though I were an adult. She told me my mother loved me very much, even if it did not seem obvious to me. She told me my mother had had a difficult time with *their* mother. "It was like Mom was jealous of Barbara," Aunt Fran had said. "And as far as she was concerned, Barbara couldn't do anything right, not one thing. My mother was all right to me, but it was very bad, the way she treated Barbara. It broke her spirit. Your mother does the best she can. You have to realize that people have reasons for the way they behave. All I can say is it's lucky your mother met your father. I don't know what she would have done without him. I love her with all my heart, but I couldn't save her like your father did."

It had been easy to believe my grandmother had been cruel to my mother; my memories of that grandmother were not good ones either. There had been about her a sense of constant disapproval. You could not touch her white porcelain poodle with the little puppies chained to it. You had to take your shoes off before you came into the house. If you drank from anything but a glass, you were a heathen. Once, in her bathroom, I'd seen a douche bag hanging from the shower rod. When I'd asked my grandmother what it was, she'd whisked it away angrily, saying, "What is the matter with you? What kind of person would ask about such things?"

When I was around five, I'd been alone with her one day; I don't remember why. But I'd come upon her when she was staring at herself in the mirror, and I was startled by the look of relaxed pleasure on her face. When she'd seen me, she turned around and regarded me with her usual expression, a half smile that was not really a smile. It was the forced pleasantry of the overburdened saleswoman who asks how she can help when what she really wants is just to go home. "What is it, Laura?" she'd asked. "It" wasn't anything; I'd just been wandering around the house. I'd simply wanted to be by her. But with my grandmother, there had to be an agenda. If you were doing nothing, you were up to no good.

The only time she touched us kids was when we were leaving— then we got a quick hug, her face directed away from us. It was like being pressed to a wall. I'd known she was warmer to Aunt Fran's children, and for a while it had bothered me. But soon enough I gave up on her altogether; we all did, and Steve and I always made vicious fun of her in the backseat every time we drove home from her house. Caroline laughed at what we said, but she wouldn't join in. Neither of our parents ever reprimanded us for our behavior at those times; rather, their relaxed posture seemed to suggest they condoned it.

My grandmother died when I was twelve, just nine months after her husband, who was really nothing more than a shadowy presence. At her funeral, I'd played hangman with Steve. As far as I was concerned, my only grandparents were my father's parents. My mother had wept for days after her mother's death, and when I'd asked her why she'd said, "Now there's no chance of anything changing. Do you understand? I'm not sorry to lose her, as she was. I'm grieving for what can never be. I'm grieving for *me*."

Now, before anyone could ask how my father was, Aunt Fran put down her magazine and said, "He's absolutely fine. The tests don't show a thing. They're going to keep him overnight just as a precaution. He can go home tomorrow."

I slumped onto an orange plastic sofa. "Oh, good. Good." Again, the image of my mother in her robe. *I told you.*

"I'm going to go talk to the nurses," Caroline said, and Steve told her to wait, he'd go with her.

"I was sure something really terrible had happened," I told Aunt Fran. "I was really sure."

"Not at all. Your mother said he ate some hot peppers last night. He can't really do that anymore, but he just won't quit."

"Mom shouldn't buy them then."

"She didn't. He did!"

I smiled and moved over a bit so Pete could fit beside me.

"I think I'm going to run home for a while," Aunt Fran said. "Want me to take the kids back to your mom's house?"

I looked over at Anthony, who hated hospitals and had ventured no farther than the entryway to the lounge, and at Hannah, sitting nervously at the edge of a chair, her empty cheese curd container still in her hand. "What do you think, guys?" I said. "You want to go back to Grandma's?"

"We'll stay if you want us to," Anthony said, and I could hear the plea in the back of his brain: *Say no.*

"I guess they don't really need to be here," I told Pete. "Why don't you go too? You might as well take them back to the fair."

"Can we?" Hannah asked.

"I think maybe we should stay for just a while," Pete said.

"Well, go in and see him if you want," Aunt Fran said. "But really, he's fine. He's mostly embarrassed. Sitting there in that silly gown."

"I'll be here," I told Pete. "Caroline and Steve will, too. You go ahead. There's no point in all of us hanging around."

He stood, his hands in his pockets, deliberating. Then, "All right." He kissed the top of my head. "I'll see you later. I'm going to go back to the fair and eat some more of the stuff that will put *me* in here next."

As soon as they left, Caroline and Steve came back into the waiting room. "Only one visitor at a time," Caroline said. "Mom's in there with him, but she said she'd be out in a minute."

"I'll go in next," I said.

"How come you get to go first?" Steve asked.

"Because I'm the oldest."

He flopped down onto a chair. "Right. I knew you were going to say that."

"Then why did you ask?"

"I just wanted to hear you say it again. Warms my heart. Brings back a lot of happy memories."

My mother came into the room and nodded to us. She looked exhausted: face wan, lines pronounced. Her hair had not been combed; it was in the same messy twist that it was this morning. I stared at her in some removed kind of fascination: I was trying to remember if I'd ever seen her go outside the house this way. As though she was aware of my thoughts, she reached up to push back the sides of her hair, to tighten her pearl studs. "I must look a fright. I left the house without doing anything."

"I doubt they'll take points off for your appearance, Mom," Caroline said.

"My appearance matters to me."

"Well, I guess we all know that."

"Stop, Caroline!" I exploded.

"Never mind," my mother said. "We're all a little edgy, that's all."

"I'm going in to see him." I walked down the short hall to the intensive care unit. Inside, the lights were low. Two nurses sat at the desk, working at computers. One looked up and smiled at me, and I said I was there to see my father.

"His name?"

"Oh," I said. "Right. Stan Meyer."

"Mr. Meyer is right here," the nurse said, and opened the door to one of the small rooms. My father was dozing, snoring lightly. I sat quietly in the chair beside his bed and looked around at all the equipment, most of which I'd only seen on television. Three moving lines of glowing green ran across a small monitor screen. There was an IV dripping into my father's arm, a bruised area around the place where the needle was inserted. I could see one of the electrodes on his chest; they'd shaved the hair off around it. On his thick wrist was a plastic name band, and for some reason the sight of this really bothered me. He could be anyone in a hospital. Therefore, anything could happen to him. I thought of a friend who'd lost her father recently, how she sat in the chair beside his unconscious form and told him she forgave him everything and that she hoped he forgave her too. How, moments after that, she'd watched him die.

I changed my position in my chair, cleared my throat. Then, "Dad?" I whispered.

His eyelids fluttered, then opened. He stared at me, blinked. "Oh, hi, Laura. I was dreaming. I was home, outside, painting the fence." He smiled. "Isn't this is a kicker? That's the last time I'll have those jalepeños."

"What happened, Dad?"

"Well, it's the damnedest thing. I ate a few last night, and then a few hours later I woke up and I was so dizzy. Then this morning, my arm went numb—your mother says I was lying on it. But I got all dizzy again too, and kind of scared, I must admit, so I called nine-one-one and they sent an ambulance. Anyway, the doc told me the good news, which is that it doesn't look like it's my heart. Might be what they call a TIA, a ministroke, but I can come back next week and get checked out for that."

His speech was a bit slurred, his mouth dry. I felt sorry for him, lying there with a half-full urinal hanging off the bedside rail—he was normally a very fastidious man. Then it came to me how lucky I was, to be feeling sorry for him because he was in a hospital bed and not walking the fairgrounds with us. He was fine; he'd go home to-morrow. So many others had been faced with so much tragedy—our family had been remarkably lucky.

"You know," I said, "you're messing up our amazing track record."

"What do you mean?"

"Nobody's ever been hospitalized in our family except for child-birth."

He nodded slowly, then said, "Well, that's not exactly true."

"Really?"

"It was . . . something happened a long time ago that I never told you kids about. I wasn't sure I should. But I was lying here after I first came in, and I thought, My God, this could be it. I could never make it out of here. And all of a sudden . . . well, I just wanted to say so much to all of you. I wanted to apologize to you kids for keeping some things from you. I wish I hadn't done that. It took coming in here for me to realize that. And yet now there's nothing wrong, I don't know if it's a good idea to tell you after all, to dig up such old bones." He smiled. "You know what I mean? Maybe it's better just to let things be."

"What are you talking about, Dad?" *Medication?* I thought. *Is he confused? Should I tell the nurse?*

But then he smiled, his old self, and reached out to touch my hand. "I don't know. I just don't know if it's right. And yet if something comes to you so strongly when you think you might be dying, shouldn't you go ahead and take care of it when you're alive?"

"Take care of what?"

"Of . . . apologizing, I guess."

"But for what?"

He hesitated for a moment, then smiled. "You know what, honey? It was a long time ago. I don't know. Forget it." He sat up straighter in his bed. "Is your mother still out there?"

For a moment I thought about pressing him to tell me what he was going to say, then decided against it. I'd talk to him about it later, when he came home. It couldn't be that important, if he'd never mentioned it before now.

"Yeah, Mom's out there. Aunt Fran left, and I sent Pete and the kids back to the fair."

"Good. I'm coming home tomorrow, I'll go with you then. But maybe I'll lay off the fried food."

"Okay." I stood up to move beside him, kissed his forehead. "I love you," I said, and he answered, "You're my girl," which was what he always said when I told him I loved him.

"Want me to send Mom in?"

He nodded, closed his eyes. "Tell her not to be offended if I'm sleeping. I'm so sleepy."

When I got back to the lounge, Caroline and Steve were sitting together on one of the sofas.

"Where's Mom?" I asked, and Steve said, "Gone out with Aunt Fran. She'll be back in an hour or so."

"Well, he looks fine," I said. "He's sleeping now."

Caroline closed the magazine she'd been reading. "Let's go to the cafeteria. I need coffee."

Steve said, "I'm too full."

Caroline said, "Just come, okay?"

He looked quickly at me, shoved his hands in his pockets, and we all headed for the elevator as though it were a gangplank.

# 9

"YOU KNOW I WANT TO TALK TO YOU BOTH," CAROLINE said. "It might as well be now." She was nervous; her hands were clenched tightly before her.

We were sitting at a small round table, off by itself. The cafeteria was all but empty. But Caroline's voice was so low I could hardly hear her.

"*Now?*" Steve asked.

"Do you mind? I mean, we're here."

Steve and I looked at each other and then sat quietly, waiting for her to begin.

Finally, she said, "All right. I was at a friend's house, not long ago. She had some new perfume, and she was telling me about how she always let her husband pick out her perfume, because her mother told her that that and good cooking were ways to keep your man happy. And then she started telling me all these other things her mother told her, most of them funny but some of them really wise, and I started trying to think about what Mom had told *me*. And I realized she'd never told me anything."

She looked up from her coffee at me, then at Steve. He was staring straight ahead, probably trying very hard not to drum his fingers on the table.

"I don't know what you mean," I said.

"I mean she never told me *anything*. Like . . . about how to iron, or sew, or cook." I rolled my eyes at this last—who would want to learn to cook like our mother?—but Caroline saw me and said, "*Or* about fashion. Or how to talk to boys. Or girls! And when I started thinking of that, I realized—"

"Caroline," Steve said.

"What?"

"Is this going to be . . . I mean, are you going to tell us about all the injustices you suffered at the hands of our terrible, terrible mother?"

"Steve," I said.

"What?"

"Let her talk."

"She can talk. I'm just asking what this is *about*."

Caroline leaned forward, spoke earnestly. "I want to know something, Steve. I wonder if you can tell me about one time when you saw some tenderness in her. Let's just start there."

"In Mom?"

"Yeah."

"Well . . . lots of times."

"Such as?"

He slumped back in his chair and looked around the room, impatient. "I don't know, like when I got hurt and stuff. Or sick."

"What did she do then?"

"Look, Caroline. I know you've got problems with Mom. You always did. But I don't want to sit around and talk about my relationship with her. I don't have any problem, okay? So if you want to talk about it, you need to talk about you. But just say it, and don't make such a big fucking stageplay out of it!"

"You know what, Steve?" She smiled bitterly, started to speak, then stopped. "Never mind. What a dumb idea, to think I could talk to you. You're not here. You've never been here. You avoid thinking about anything; you just buy big-boy toys and—"

Steve stood and pushed his chair hard under the table. "I figured when you said you wanted to talk to me and Laura, it'd be some crap like this. You know what I think, Caroline? I think you should grow up. You're fifty years old, for Christ's sake."

"Fifty-one, thank you. And excuse me, *I* should grow up?"

"I'm going back upstairs," he said. "Dad's in the hospital. That's why we're here, remember? Believe it or not, we're involved in something here that has nothing to do with you."

"Steve," I said, but it was too late. He walked away.

Caroline watched him disappear out the swinging door. "I don't know what I was thinking. He's never cared anything about me."

"That's not true," I said.

"It is. I shouldn't mind, really. I should be used to it."

"He does care about you. He doesn't like to talk about things, that's all. I mean, you ask him about tenderness . . . he's not like that. He's a guy, only worse. And—well, Dad *is* in the hospital."

"I know he is, but he's fine! And I just figured, since we were all here together, now was as good a time as any. I needed something. I really needed something from him, and I thought I'd ask."

"Well, ask then. You've got to be direct with him."

She looked down. "It's hard."

I wanted so much to say, tiredly, Everything is hard for you, Caroline. But I didn't. I looked out the window, at the birds flying free, and said, "Well, ask me, then. I'm here. Ask me."

She nodded, took a deep breath in, blew it out. "One thing I want to know is what I was asking Steve. Really. I want to know if you can remember anything . . . tender that Mom ever did."

"Okay, so you mean being hugged and kissed, stuff like that?"

"No. I know she did that sometimes, but it was always . . . it felt like it was for show. It was always in front of someone else. No, I mean other things. Things she did just for you, without an audience. Like . . . did she ever just sit on your bed and talk to you?"

I thought back and tried to remember. Truthfully, I couldn't recall anything like that. And so I said, "No. I don't think she did. But, see, I don't think I minded."

She pushed her cup aside, leaned in toward me. "All right. Let me ask you this, then. Do you remember her ever being overtly cruel to you?"

"Oh, Caroline. Weren't you, as a mother? Weren't you ever cruel to Eva?"

"Yes. Yes, I was, I'm sure. But not . . . it wasn't intentional. It wasn't dispassionate or calculated."

"What does that mean? You think Mom was intentionally cruel to you?" I was beginning to wish I'd walked out with Steve. Given my mother's background, it was understandable that she wasn't particularly cuddly, that there was about her a certain dark mystery. But she had never raised a hand to us, had rarely even raised her voice.

"She was. And she crippled me in ways I can't even . . ." She closed her eyes, rubbed her forehead. Then she looked at me, her green eyes hard. "This is part of the deal I made with the therapist, okay? I promised I'd talk to you and Steve. If I can just get some sort of acknowledgment—"

"Caroline. I'm sorry for what you've been feeling. I am. I know your life growing up was difficult; you were a very sensitive kid. And . . . highly imaginative in ways that I think hurt you. I think you hurt yourself because of the way you seemed to dwell on sad things. I thought you'd have to be hospitalized after we saw *Bambi*." I smiled at her, but she didn't smile back.

I leaned in closer, chose my words carefully. I didn't want her to know what I was thinking, which was that she was a liar. I had to find a gentler way to say that—and to think it. Deluding herself; that might be a better way of saying it. I'd think of something.

For the time being, I just said, "Look. I understand you're going through a lot of pain now. I wish I could help—I'm worried about you. But you're talking in circles. I think we should go back upstairs. We can talk more about this later, I promise." I stood, picked up my purse. Caroline stayed seated.

"Are you coming?"

She didn't look at me. But she said, "One time, when I was about seven, she came into my room and I was lying on the bed, naked—I wanted to see how it felt to have all my skin against that silky coverlet I used to have. And she yanked me off the bed and shoved me up against the wall and said, 'Shame on you! Shame on you!' and shook me so hard I thought my neck would snap." She swallowed. "Then she put her hands around my throat and wouldn't let go. She didn't squeeze, but she wouldn't let go. Finally, I bit her. Then she let go."

I sat back down at the table.

"That's not the only thing she did like that. She told me it was my fault, that I made her do these things to me. I believed her." She laughs. "And you know what? Telling you all this now, I can feel some part of me still believing it."

"Caroline, is this really true?" She looked up quickly at me, and I said, "I'm sorry. I'm sorry, but is it? Tell me honestly, now."

Caroline laughed, a short, bitter sound. "Right." She slid out of her chair and walked quickly away, and I cast about for the right thing to do. Call her back? Call her names? The truth was, I didn't believe her. I couldn't imagine my mother doing such things. Then it came to me that maybe what I couldn't imagine was my not knowing. And by extension, of course, my not doing anything about it.

I remembered a winter night when Caroline and I were perhaps eight and ten. We were lying together in my bed, the blankets pulled up high over us. We'd had a flashlight that we were using as a microphone, and we'd been playing some sort of game where I was the host and Caroline was a glamorous movie star who was being interviewed about her glamorous life. "And how many Christmas presents did you get this year?" I'd asked, and Caroline had said, in a pleasingly affected voice, "Oh, my heavens, so many; too many to count. I got a horse, a Tennessee Walker. And I got a jewelry box full of diamond necklaces. And I got toilet paper made of satin and silk." We'd giggled, I remember, and then, all of a sudden, she'd turned to me and said, "I wish I could die." At first, I was confused, thinking the "star" was talking. But then I had understood it was Caroline, speaking for herself. "Don't you?"

"Don't I what?" I was beginning to be afraid of her. I could feel a coldness rising up my spine. I hated how her bangs were cut crookedly, how pale she was, the bruise-colored circles beneath her eyes.

"Don't you wish you could die now?" she whispered. "Just like this?"

"*No!*" I'd said, and she stopped smiling. I think she was genuinely surprised at my response. "Why would you wish a thing like that?"

"Because. We'd go to heaven if we died right now. If we live much longer, we probably won't. Our sins will get bigger and bigger." She had turned on her side, facing me. "Anyway, I don't like it here. I don't really like it."

I'd lain still for a moment. Then I'd said, "Go back to your own bed. You're creepy. You're so creepy. I'm telling what you said."

"No, you won't," she'd said. And she'd been right. I'd always let her bear her peculiar burdens alone.

IN THE ICU WAITING ROOM, Steve was hunched over a magazine, one leg draped over the arm of his chair. "Where's Caroline?" I asked.

"Don't know. Don't care." He looked up at me, shrugged.

"She just told me something really incredible." I repeated for him the story Caroline had told me about our mother. When I finished, he straightened in his seat, put down the magazine. "Jesus."

"I know." I supposed he was thinking the same things I had: How did I miss this? How could the mother I had be the mother who did such things?

The door to the lounge opened and a somber-faced woman entered and sat on the chair closest to the door. She was wearing blue-jean shorts and a sleeveless white blouse, a pair of sneakers with no socks. She carried a large straw purse, and lying across the top of it was a battered teddy bear. She nodded at us, her eyes shining with tears.

"Hi," I said softly.

"Hi." She picked up a magazine, stared determinedly at it, shivered slightly in the air-conditioning. The room was rich with a unique kind of silence that was full of things that needed to be expressed but couldn't be. I looked at Steve, pointed to the door, and he followed me out.

"She must have a child being admitted," I said. "My God. Can you imagine your child being in the ICU? I'd go crazy if one of my children had to be in there."

"Where do you think Caroline went? Speaking of children."

"Beats me."

He leaned against the wall, crossed his arms. "Well, now I feel like a real jerk. But do you think . . . don't get mad, okay? But do you believe her?"

"Oh. . . . No. Probably not. That's why she left, because I made her feel like I don't believe her. I'm sure it's not literally true; Caroline always exaggerates everything so much. But if she—"

The elevator dinged, the doors parted, and we saw my mother coming down the hall. I watched her, trying to see if there was something about her that would confirm or deny what Caroline had just told me. But she was only my mother, the woman signing my report cards, applauding my first ride on my bike without training wheels, chopping onions with a match held between her teeth to keep from crying, carpet-sweeping the living room, standing at the foot of my bed to hold Anthony as a newborn, her hand protectively cradling his head with great skill and care. I had to talk to Caroline's husband. If not her therapist.

My mother had changed clothes, combed her hair, regained her regal bearing. But as she came closer, I saw a look on her face I couldn't quite decipher. "I just saw Caroline on the way out," she said. Neither Steve nor I said anything back. "She's going home, she said. She's not coming back."

"Ah," I said, as though it made perfect sense. As though it were what I'd been waiting for.

"I do not understand that child," my mother said. "I never have and I never will."

"She's going home to her house?" I asked.

My mother nodded. "I'm going in to see your father. I'm going to tell him something came up for Caroline at work that she's got to go home and take care of. He doesn't need to know she didn't care enough to see him come out of the hospital tomorrow."

"Well, she'll be over, I'm sure," I said.

My mother looked at me, angry. "You know what I mean."

"I'll tell you what," I said. "I'll go over there. I'll go to her house and talk to her."

"You want me to come?" Steve asked, and I shook my head no. I pressed the button for the elevator. "Tell Pete where I went. I'll see you later."

# 10

ANTHONY WAS RIGHT: I HAD TO GET A CELL PHONE. I
was standing at a bank of phones in a hall adjacent to a
road-stop restaurant. I was squeezed between two callers:
one a young dark-haired woman hunched over the receiver who apparently was attempting to have a secretive
conversation, the other a wiry trucker sucking hard on a
cigarette and yelling that he couldn't possibly arrive on
time, no, he could not possibly arrive on time; where was
Phyllis, put Phyllis on the line, she was the only one in the
whole place that knew what was really going on, where
was goddamn Phyllis?

On the way to Caroline's, I had suddenly wanted to
talk to my friend Maggie, to hear a voice from home saying that everything there is fine, everything there is still
the same. I thought if I could hear her voice, I would be
better able to visualize my house: the late-afternoon sun-
shine that makes an ellipse of light against the living room

wall, the folded piles of fabric on my sewing table, the wooden spoons standing at attention in my kitchen, the doors to the kids' rooms open halfway. I'd be able to see the hydrangea blossoms heavy on their bushes in the backyard, the treehouse that Hannah reads in. In addition to comforting myself with such images, I wanted to tell Maggie what had gone on, to ask her what she thought I should do. She was very good in situations like this.

But she wasn't there.

If there is one thing I can't stand, it's being in dire need of talking to a girlfriend and having her husband answer the phone and say she's not there. Then you have two problems: the person you so much need to connect with is not available, *and* you have to rearrange your emotions to converse with a man. There is not a thing in the world wrong with Maggie's husband. Doug is affable and generous and a good cook to boot. But he is of the Y-chromosome school of emotional receptivity. So instead of trying to tell him what was going on, I took in a deep breath, turned down the anxiety flame, and said, "Okay! Well, I'll just try later." And then, in as friendly and even a tone of voice as I could muster, I said, "So what are you doing home in the middle of the day?"

"It's Saturday," he said.

And I said, "Oh. Right."

When I hung up, I stood for a moment in front of the phone, my arms crossed. It occurred to me to call Caroline and leave her a message letting her know I was on my way, that I'd be there soon after she arrived. But I didn't.

I got back in the car, started the engine, then turned it off. I rolled down the window, rested my forehead against the steering wheel, and closed my eyes. I'd only wanted to come home and go to the fair, just like always. Instead, I felt like I'd walked into a room where the door had slammed shut behind me, then disappeared altogether.

\* \* \*

A FEW BLOCKS AWAY FROM CAROLINE'S HOUSE, I pulled into a 7-Eleven. I'd decided I did want to call before I showed up; it seemed only fair. But when I tried her number, I got her voice mail. It was possible that she hadn't arrived yet, but that seemed unlikely. It seemed more appropriate to imagine her lying in bed, fully clothed down to her shoes but under the covers, the way she sometimes was found after a bad day in high school.

I bought a package of Twinkies, always our favorite as kids, and a *National Enquirer. A little joke, ha-ha; here you go, Caroline, now let's finish talking and get this over with.*

I pulled into her driveway and parked behind her car. Caroline lived in a beautiful old Victorian that she'd bought when it was a wreck—raccoons had been living there. But she'd loved the bones of the house and saw its potential immediately. Now it was the nicest place on the block.

I went up to the front door and knocked quickly, then tried opening it. Locked. I called her name once, twice. Nothing. I rang the doorbell; then, shading my eyes, I looked in the uncurtained windows of the living room. And there she was, sitting in a chair with her purse at her feet, staring right back at me.

"Open the door," I said.

She didn't move.

Louder, I said, "Caroline! Open the door!"

She got up slowly, came to the door, and opened it. Then she went back to her chair.

I came in, closed the door, and moved to the sofa near her. The mantel clock ticked loudly in the silence. Ticked questioningly, I felt, speaking for Caroline: *What–do–you–want?* I leaned forward, touched her hand lightly. "Hey."

Nothing.

"I brought you something." I pulled the Twinkies out of the bag, the *National Enquirer.*

She wouldn't look.

"Want a Twinkie?" I asked, and then realized the stupidity of it. The unkindness, really. "Caroline," I said gently. "What's going on?"

"I tried to tell you. You called me a liar."

"I did not call you a liar."

She looked over at me, smiled bitterly.

"I didn't call you a liar! I simply asked you if you were *sure*. Come on, you told me this incredible thing, and I just was having trouble . . . I mean, you seem to think you can just—"

The phone rang and I stopped talking, grateful for the interruption. But Caroline made no move to answer it.

"Aren't you going to get that?"

"No."

The phone rang twice more, stopped, then immediately started again.

"Maybe it's important," I said.

"I don't care. I'm not going to answer the phone."

"Well, then, I will."

I started to get up and she said, "Don't! This is not your house. You are not allowed to use the phone."

"Caroline. Dad's in the hospital. It could be about him."

"Dad is fine." The phone stopped ringing again.

"I'm calling home, goddammit." I went into the kitchen, dialed my parents' number. My mother answered immediately. "It's me," I said.

"Yes?"

"I'm here at Caroline's and the phone rang and we didn't . . . we missed it. It wasn't you, was it?"

"No, it wasn't. What's going on there? Is everything all right?"

I looked toward the living room. "Yes. It's fine. We're just talking."

Caroline came into the kitchen, took the phone from me and hung it up. She turned the ringer off. Then, facing me, she said, "I told you not to answer the phone. I don't want to talk to anyone. Including you." She headed upstairs, and I heard a door slam. I stood still for a minute, then angrily followed her up. I opened the door to her bedroom and found her sitting on the edge of the unmade bed, her hands folded in her lap. Her closet door was open; I could see that Bill's clothes were gone. It was true, then; they were separated.

My anger faded and I sat beside her for some time, saying nothing. Finally, she looked over at me, and I put my arm around her. It occurred to me that this might be the first time I'd ever done this. Her body was stiff, unyielding. Actually, mine was too. Some part of me wanted to stop then, to get up and leave. Drive back to my parents' house and talk to my children about what they did that day, sit in the backyard that night to watch the crayon-colored fireworks that would be shot off from the fairgrounds. I wanted to shrug off all the things Caroline had said in the way I might an unpleasant encounter in a parking lot. But I saw the wrongness in that.

"I'll wait," I said finally. "Okay? I'll wait right here until you're ready. And then I'll listen to you. I promise." She nodded, and she might as well have been transformed into that sad and mysterious little girl who shared a family with me but who didn't belong—not then and not now, either.

*It is taken on Easter Sunday. My mother, a study in per-*
*fumed agitation, had hustled Caroline and me outside the*
*house before church, saying we had to have our picture taken*
*together in our identical outfits because our paternal grand-*
*mother had (sigh) insisted. Nana had sent us dresses made*
*out of a filmy powder-blue-and-white polka-dotted fabric, as*
*well as beribboned hats and white patent leather purses. We*
*have been made to hold hands, and the expression beneath*
*my smile is pained; I am holding only Caroline's thumb,*
*rather in the way you might hold a thumb you found on the*
*ground. Caroline smiles her usual sad smile and holds her*
*other hand up to her eye, her fingers fashioning a grip around*
*her own imaginary camera. She, the one being pho-*
*tographed, is the one recording the truer image.*

*I remember that the moment the photo was taken, I*
*dropped Caroline's hand and ran toward the car. "Wait for*
*me!" she called, but I did not. I claimed a coveted seat by the*
*window and then wiped the hand that had touched Caroline*
*against the skirt of my new dress, first front, then back, over*

and over again. I think I might have used my purse to try to block anyone from seeing, but I can't be sure that is not just my horrified adult self, editing.

Well, yes. That is what it is. Because now I remember that when Caroline got in the car she was carrying both her own purse and mine, which I'd left behind. She held mine out to me, all hope, saying excitedly, "Here, Laura, you forgot this! You forgot our new purse!" "I don't want it," I said, staring straight ahead. "I don't even like it." It was the possessive pronoun I objected to. From the corner of my eye, I saw her hesitate, then put the purse gently down on the seat between us. I saw her straighten it just the tiniest bit, then struggle to move herself into a comfortable position without disturbing anything.

# 11

CAROLINE AND I WERE SITTING OUTSIDE ON HER BACK porch steps, eating salad and drinking Diet Pepsi. "What I really want is potato chips and Lipton Onion Soup dip," Caroline said. "It's the fair. It makes you want only junk food."

"We can have that," I said. "Let's go and get some."

"No." She reached down to slap her ankle. "Damn mosquitoes."

I looked at my watch. I'd been here now for almost two hours. "Caroline—"

"I know." She finished her Pepsi and set the can down carefully, as though it were made of crystal. This opposed to my having crushed my own can with one hand, after which I'd burped and said, "See that? Supergirl."

"All right," Caroline said. "I'll try to tell you. I'll try again. Maybe it would help if I give you some background.

"A few months ago, I'd come to the point where I was beginning to feel paralyzed about doing anything for myself. It's always been hard for me to take . . . well, to take. But it became extreme. Bill and I make good money, we own the house and our cars, I pay my credit card bills in full every month, and yet I find myself standing in a store holding up a blouse and wondering why I'm even looking at it, because I know I won't buy it for myself."

"Well, I do that too, Caroline. I think everyone does. You look at something you want to buy and feel guilty that you're getting it for yourself. Especially women; we think it's selfish if—"

"But it was more than that. It was this feeling that . . . it was the feeling that the world is not for me. Life. It's not for me."

I stared out across her backyard, watched two yellow butterflies chasing each other in circles. Look at that, I wanted to say, but didn't. Of course I didn't. Inside, I could hear my child voice saying, "Come *on*. Let's *go*."

"I kept feeling worse and worse—I couldn't work, I couldn't sleep, I couldn't read—I'd just look at the same sentence over and over. Things were terrible with Bill, and finally he'd just had it. He couldn't help me and he couldn't listen to me anymore, and frankly I don't blame him. He said he wanted to be apart for a while, that then maybe I'd get some help. He'd been asking me to go and see someone for a long time, but I couldn't.

"When he left, though, I finally did call a shrink. One of the things she told me to do was to find something to do with my evenings, to make sure I went out at least once a week. I signed up for a free class, memoir writing—something they were offering at the library. And it was the oddest thing. I found I couldn't write my real life. I could only make things up. I felt afraid of telling a single fact, as though I couldn't be depended on to get it right. Finally, I thought, Well, you know where you *lived*, for God's sake. You know what the *house* where you grew up was like. And I'd start to write about it, but then I'd stop and I'd think, Wait. *Were* there trees along the boulevard in front? *Was* my bedspread blue? I talked to my therapist about this, week after week, and suddenly I realized where it was all coming from, all this self-doubt, all this censorship.

"We'd talked one day about the concept of shame, and I told her that every time I heard that word, I had a visceral reaction to it: I could feel my stomach clench, my heart start to race. She said, 'Well, let's explore that.' And I sat there on her couch and I all of a sudden felt this rush of something *awful* coming, this freight train of emotion. I just came completely apart, started bawling. And then I began remembering things that happened to me. Triggered memories, they call it. They just kept popping up."

I was quiet for a long time, thinking. Then I said, "I wish, for your sake, that I could remember her doing something like that. But I can't think of one time she ever behaved that way. Which is not to say I don't believe you, Caroline. I just don't remember anything."

"She didn't do the worst stuff in front of you," Caroline said. "I know that. But what I wanted to know from you and Steve is if you remember . . . smaller things. General things. If you can, it will help me to keep going. I just want to know that you saw something too. Do you understand? I don't doubt what happened, but I seem to need something else to help me do something about it."

I leaned back on my elbows and stared up at the sky. It was getting dark out. Clouds were stretched thin as gossamer, and stars were appearing behind them. Whole galaxies above us, whole galaxies within us.

I thought back to our growing-up years, trying to remember a time when Caroline was purposefully slighted by my mother. But I really couldn't. I'd been aware of the fact that, after a certain point, Caroline's attitude toward my mother switched from idolatry to contempt. But that had happened with all of us when we went through adolescence; with Caroline, it had just been more dramatic—no surprise there. Finally, I said, "I guess I didn't pay much attention, Caroline."

Saying that, I suddenly wondered what it really meant. Why was I so firmly entrenched in my own world? What went on in our house that made me look so determinedly away from everything but my own fantasies? Was it possible the shrink I saw in college was at least partially right, that something wrong in my family made me seek comfort elsewhere? But couldn't everyone look back at life as a child and start blaming their parents for what was wrong with them? Frankly, I was really, really tired of that song.

"It's kind of hard, Caroline, trying to remember anything from so long ago. I mean, stuff from my life alone, to say nothing of yours. I remember specific moments, but whole years are just . . . lost."

She nodded. "Yeah."

"But why do you need Steve's and my corroboration anyway? You said you know this happened."

"I guess it's that I need to feel I have allies in my brother and my sister, that I'm not alone in what I need to do. If I don't confront Mom—and Dad too, I guess—I'll never get past all this. I have to tell them about what I remember. And that it was wrong."

"Oh, God."

"Laura, you don't know.

"She came into my room one Saturday. I had just started third grade, and I was sitting at the window, looking out at the leaves. It was fall, and they were really beautiful. She asked me why I didn't go outside. I said I wanted to be in. I said, Look at the leaves, they're so pretty and they're dying. She got sort of impatient and started messing around with the stuff in my room, rearranging it. Then she said I had to go out, that I was just mooning around and there was no reason for it, it was a perfectly beautiful day. I said again I didn't want to, and I asked why the leaves had to die, why did things have to die, and she grabbed my arm and started pulling me out of my room. And I remember I yelled *help*, I yelled *help* really loud, and she just went berserk. She started slapping me and kicking me and saying to shut up, just shut *up*. And then she ran into her bedroom and slammed the door and started sobbing—I could hear her all the way in my room. I went and knocked at her door, and then I went in, and she was lying on her side holding a pillow up against her stomach. She said I made her do these things, why did I make her do these things? I remember I tried to get on the bed beside her, I was so sorry, and she lifted up her head and said in this awful, low voice, '*Get out of here.*' I went back to my room and stayed until dinnertime, and when I came out it was like nothing happened."

"But . . . where was I that day?"

"You were gone somewhere," Caroline said. "Probably over at a friend's house; you were a good girl with a lot of friends. You were forever going over somewhere and baking with someone and then bringing home stuff for the family. Look what I made! Little Miss Martha."

I pictured myself standing in Sally Burke's kitchen, laughing and licking chocolate-chip cookie dough from beaters while Caroline sat at the edge of her bed staring at her hands, afraid to move. "Oh, Caroline. I don't see how you can stand any of us. I can't believe I was oblivious to all this. That we all were. Didn't anybody ever even— why didn't you tell Dad?"

She shook her head. "Well, as I told you, Mom had me convinced that the bad things she did to me were my fault. She truly did. I was so ashamed of the fact that there was something in me that made her behave in this terrible way. I knew she wasn't like that to you or Steve, so it had to be my fault. I did try to tell Dad one day, but it was useless. You know how it is; you can't say anything bad about Mom to Dad. I'm sure he thought I was making it up. He probably thought I'd gotten in trouble for something and had been mildly punished in some way or another, then had exaggerated wildly about what happened. I *was* prone to drama, as you recall."

I refrained from correcting the tense. "But . . . didn't you have marks or something?"

"I had bruises every now and then. But so did you. Only yours came from another place."

"Well, I just . . . I have to say, Caroline, if all that had happened to me, I think I'd just walk away from our parents. Cut off relations."

"Don't be so sure. I have a friend, a guy I met at my group counseling session. And once a month, on the first day of the month, he goes to see his father, who was remarkably abusive—both physically and emotionally. He goes even though he knows that every time it'll be like getting shot in the heart. His father insults him for a while and then basically ignores him. Eddie knows what he's headed for, but he can't stop going. And I understand why. It has to do with himself, what Eddie's giving *himself*."

"But what *is* he giving himself? He's just sticking his finger into the light socket! There are such things as toxic parents."

"Yes, but . . . let me ask you something. Do you like your feet?"

I pulled my bare feet away self-consciously. I thought she knew that I hated my feet: I have little toes that look like cornichons, according to Pete. And that's a kind analogy. More like slugs, Anthony says. And my fat big toe curves over as though it's trying to commiserate with the little toe. "No."

"Ever had a pedicure?"

"No!"

"Why not? It could help."

"Because then I'd have to show someone my feet close up for a long time."

"Well, why don't you cut them off?"

"My feet?"

"Yeah."

I half smiled. "What are you talking about, Caroline?"

"You've always hated your feet. Why don't you just cut them off?"

Fine. I would play along. "I need them to stand on. To walk."

She nodded. "Exactly."

I sat still for a moment, then said, "All right. I get it."

"I need Mom to admit to what she did, so I can forgive her. Then I can stand. Then I can walk to where I need to go, if I may extend the metaphor."

"Right. I understand." I leaned back on my elbows. "You know one of the things that's really hard about this, Caroline? That you waited for so *long*."

"Yeah. I met a woman who told me about how she finally came to love her mother, who made our mother look like Mother Teresa. She said she was able to love her mother when she began to get more sure of herself. And you know when that was?"

"When?"

"When she was fifty-nine."

I laughed. "Okay. Okay. So what now, then? How do I help?"

"Well, you can start by trying to believe me."

"I do believe you!"

She stood, stretched. "I appreciate your saying that. But here's what I know. Partly you believe me, and partly you don't." I started to protest and she held up her hand to stop me. "That's why you asked me about marks."

I looked away. She was right.

Her voice softened. "It's okay. It's hard, I know. And I know this will all take time. Everything about it will take a long time. I just hope that in the end . . ."

"I hope so too, Caroline."

"We should go in before we get bit up any more."

"Let's go to the grocery store," I said.

"What do you need?"

"I want to help you get something *you* need: chips and dip. I figured we'd start small."

"I don't know if Rainbow is still open."

"I'll see." I went into the house and picked up the phone. "Hey, Caroline, you have messages on here."

"It's just Bill. He calls every night. I'll call him back later."

"He calls every night?"

"Yeah."

"Well, good. That's good, isn't it?"

Nothing.

"Caroline?"

"What."

"That's good, isn't it? That he calls every night?"

"Yeah," she said. "It's good."

I called information, then the grocery store. "They close in twenty minutes," I yelled.

Caroline came into the house, the screen door banging behind her. "Let's go!" It was the first time in so long that I'd seen her look happy. And of course it wasn't the food.

ON THE WAY BACK TO MY PARENTS' HOUSE, I thought of all Caroline had told me. When our family sat down together at dinner on a random Tuesday night, was it possible she was recovering from some sort of horrible event only hours before? What had been held in her silences?

When I was a few blocks away, I turned off the radio. I wanted to think about how much I should tell my parents. I decided on as little as possible: I'd just say Caroline would be over tomorrow afternoon, that there were some things she would like to talk about with the immediate family. I had no idea what I'd do with the kids. As much as they like the fair, they don't like to go two days in a row. I'd have to ask Pete to take them somewhere. There was no reason for him to be around during all of this. I tried not to pay attention to the pinch of resentment I felt; this wasn't how our time here was supposed to go. We were supposed to have fun.

When I pulled into the driveway, I saw the dim figures of people sitting outside. It was Pete and the kids, arranged in an intimate little semicircle, waiting for the fireworks, I supposed. I greeted them, dropped my purse, and sat on the grass before them. I pulled my knees up to my chest, rested my forehead on top of them, and drew in a long breath. I could finally relax. I looked up, smiling.

"Where have you *been*?" Anthony asked.

"Why? Did you miss me?" I rose up to kiss the top of his head multiple times, just to annoy him. His head smelled good, a yeasty smell. "Awww, did you miss me?"

He frowned, looked away.

"Laura," Pete said.

I turned toward him. "Yeah?" Then, my smile disappearing, I said, "What?" And then, as he got out of his chair and started toward me, his face full of sadness, "Oh, my God."

# 12

WHEN PETE AND I HAD FINALLY GOTTEN AROUND TO making our wills, we'd talked about what we wanted done at our funerals. He'd wanted a straight service, something dignified; I wanted something looser. I'd wanted things read by friends and relatives that would entertain and inspire: essays by Annie Dillard, poetry by Mary Oliver. I'd wanted one quilt over me, another one draped over the coffin, and the one called "Water at Night," my pride and joy, the silver and black quilt that won first prize in a national competition—I'd wanted that quilt to be given away by a raffle drawing. When everyone filed out of the church, I'd wanted James Brown to be singing "I Feel Good."

"You don't want James *Brown*," Pete had said, and I'd said, "Yes I do. I want people to think that's how it is, over yonder. That you feel good."

"Okay," he'd said, in that singsong way that meant *I think you're nuts.*

Of course when you plan your funeral, you do it thinking you won't really die. It's just a good exercise. You plan it in case you die.

You know your parents are going to die, but they are going to die later. They are going to die *sometime*. But that time will not come until you no longer need them. While you still need them, or might need them, they will have the good taste and common courtesy not to leave. This was how I'd always thought of it, I see now.

At my father's funeral I sat frozen, holding Pete's hand tightly and feeling absolutely nothing. The priest was standing at the pulpit, sharing amusing anecdotes about my father so we could all remember we were here *not to mourn a death but to celebrate a life*. Amid the sounds of sniffing and discreet nose-blowing came appreciative chuckles—appreciative or obligatory, I wasn't sure which.

Steve sat in the row ahead of us, Tessa leaning into him. On his other side sat my mother, dabbing at her eyes. At the end of our row, Caroline sat next to Bill but at a slight declarative distance from him. I looked around the church, at the dull sheen of old gold, the stained-glass windows. I thought about a quilt I'd once made out of jewel-colored douppioni silks, designed to look like stained glass. I remembered a time I'd sat beside my father when we went to midnight mass. The decorations were so beautiful, the music so rich, I'd begun to quietly weep in awe and appreciation, and my father, staring straight ahead, had reached over to take my hand: *I know.* And now the dam broke and I understood that it was true; my father had died and I was sitting here at his funeral and he would never take my hand again.

I remembered him reading to me when I had the mumps, the same battered Little Golden Book, over and over again. I remembered him bandaging my knee on a day I fell off my bike, hugging me before I left for college, walking me down the aisle on my wedding day, how his eyes filled with tears when he told Pete in as stern a voice as he could muster, "You take good care of her, now." I thought of riding high on his shoulders when I was three, him trying to teach me how to whistle, and how, when I learned, he'd given me a new dollar bill. I remembered the night someone stole my Halloween candy and I came home crying, and he went out for hours looking for some boy dressed as a skeleton. I remembered the first quilt show I had at a gallery, how he had come to the opening and walked up to everyone there, saying quietly, "Hi, how are you, I'm her father; she's my daughter; isn't she something?"

My chest heaved and a whimpering sound escaped that under other circumstances might have embarrassed me. But now, I didn't care about anything except the fact that my father had died and I had not been ready. I had not been done with him. I wanted him to come back for just half an hour, so I could say what I had saved up for another time. For later.

I thought, There was a *tag* tied to his toe.

I thought, His clothes were not folded and put on the shelf inside the metal locker, they were tossed onto the bottom of it, and his blue shirt was turned inside out.

I thought, His glasses were on the otherwise empty nightstand, and his wallet was in the otherwise empty drawer, only I thought of it this way: His little glasses. His little wallet.

I thought, He didn't know, he had no idea, he was only trying to eat his tasteless hospital dinner thinking that tomorrow night he'd be home to watch television with my mother in the family room, his simple evening pleasure. And then his cup had fallen, and coffee had run from the side of his mouth, and despite everything they tried he was gone.

I squeezed Pete's hand tighter. I thought, *Don't ever leave me, let me go first.* From the corner of my eye I saw the knees of my children. They were so old now, not really children anymore. *Stop that,* I wanted to tell them. *Hold still.*

# 13

AT MY PARENTS'—NOW MY MOTHER'S—HOUSE, THE living room was crowded with people who had come over after the funeral. I'd met so many strangers who knew my father, had talked to so many friends and relatives I'd known since I was a child, that I'd actually gotten hoarse. I went into the TV room, needing a break, and found Anthony sitting in my father's leather recliner, his knee bouncing wildly.

"Hi," I said.

"Hi." He didn't look at me. His knee slowed, stopped.

I sat in my mother's blue velvet club chair. "How are you doing, sweetheart?"

He shrugged.

"It's hard, huh?" I said. "Hard to realize that one minute he was just—"

"It's not that!"

"Oh." I sat still, waiting.

He looked at me, then quickly wiped a tear away. "It's not that he died. People *die*. It's . . . *this*. I mean, I think it's really gross, what's going on out there. People just . . . chewing their dumb sandwiches and drinking and laughing. It's not a party! How come nobody's talking about Grandpa?"

"Well, some people are. Here and there. Some people are. But I think I know how you feel. When Great-grandma died, there was a lunch in the church basement after her funeral, and I remember looking around, thinking, This could be anything *but* a funeral."

"Exactly." He looked over at me. "A celebration for someone graduating high school or something. A birthday."

"Yes. But I see it differently. I think what this is, is people just needing to do something, to keep going and not be alone. You know? What if these people didn't come back here? Then Grandma would be by herself. And she—"

"She wouldn't be alone! We're here!"

"Well, yes. We're here now. But we aren't going to be staying here. These people all live nearby."

The knee again. And then Anthony reached for the remote. "There's a good baseball game on. Why don't I just watch it?" He looked at me, eyebrows raised. "Okay?"

I didn't know if he was serious or not. "I suppose you could."

"I don't want to watch a game!"

"You could, though, and there would be nothing wrong with it. People . . . they have to find their own ways. Everybody has a different method of coping with grief, and no one way is better than another. You might *need* to watch a baseball game now. It might remind you of your normal life, of what you have to go back to. For Grandma . . . well, she needs to be reminded that people are around to help her. All these people 'eating their dumb sandwiches' will tell her that if she needs anything—"

"Yeah, and most of them won't even mean it!"

"Some of them might not. But others will." I leaned back and felt an edgy restlessness snaking through me. I needed to go outside. Later, I'd ask Pete to take a walk with me. I hadn't had a chance to be alone with him since we'd arrived, and that's what *I* needed. "It's like falling off a cliff, Anthony, when someone dies this suddenly. And these rituals we have, whatever they are—watching sports or having dinner parties, or . . . oh, I don't know, wearing a yellow tie every third Thursday—they provide some sort of support. You know what I mean? So you can watch baseball. Hannah can call her friends— Hannah *is* on the phone with Gracie, right now. And Grandma is in the kitchen peeling Saran Wrap off cold cuts and tossing salads and arranging cookies on platters instead of weeping in her darkened bedroom with the door closed. All of this—I don't know, maybe it forges a new neural pathway, almost. It helps you go on in this new situation. It teaches you how. Don't you think Grandma's heart is breaking? Of course it is. But does she honor Grandpa by collapsing into grief? Believe me, she'll do plenty of that. But for right now, I think it's better if she talks to people and accepts the gifts they can offer. No one is saying Grandpa's life didn't matter. They're just coming together to do what they can. They're providing some structure, some order, to a situation that feels out of control, especially to Grandma."

Anthony listened, biting at his lower lip. Then he stood up. "So what should I do? I'm sorry, I just don't feel like talking to strangers, answering all these dumb questions about how do I like North Dakota, I ought to play basketball, I'm so tall, blah, blah, blah. But I'd like to . . . should I maybe throw away the used paper plates?" He laughed in his harsh teenage way, embarrassed.

"I think that's a perfect thing to do."

He came over to me, put his hand on my shoulder. "And . . . are you okay, Mom? You know, I just realized . . . It was your dad!"

I smiled up at him. "I'm fine. You know what I'm mostly thinking? That I'm so lucky. To have had him, and to have you."

There, a hint of color in his face, his shoulders shifting off some discomfort. I wasn't allowed to show him much affection anymore, no matter how oblique it might be. When he was in second grade, I was allowed to kiss him before he left for school only in the coat closet, door closed. By the time he got to third grade, I got in trouble for even thinking about kissing him. Yet there are still nights when I sit at the side of his bed before he goes to sleep and we talk for a long time—about nothing, really. He lies stretched out under the covers with his hands linked behind his head, smelling of shampoo, his bedside lamp giving him a halo. "O'Conner thinks he's set for a basketball scholarship," he'll say. "Huh!" I'll say. "A scholarship! That's great." And I'll be thinking, *You've become a man, right in front of my eyes. I can't bear the thought that you'll leave soon.*

"You want me to bring you anything?" Anthony asked. "Want a sandwich or something? Cookies?"

"No, thanks. I'm fine."

Just after he left the room, Caroline came in. She sat in my father's chair, looked over at me, and sighed. "Well. That's that."

"Yeah," I said sadly.

"I mean, now nobody will ever believe me."

"Oh, my God. You—" I stared at her.

"*What*, Laura?"

I shook my head, got up from my chair, and walked out.

In the living room, I caught sight of Hannah sitting alone on the sofa, and I went to sit beside her, took her hand.

"How's Gracie?"

"Fine. She said she misses me."

"Ah. That's nice. It's nice to be missed, huh?"

"I miss Grandpa already. And I feel so sorry. Like for how I didn't do stuff for him."

"He adored you. Do you know that?"

A moment. Then she nodded.

"You did a lot for him by just being you."

"No, I didn't. I should have done way more things. Like every time we were leaving, he used to say, 'Drop me a line, kiddo!' And I hardly ever wrote him. Only about four or five times in my whole life!"

"I guess none of us ever does all that we might have for one another. But I know this: You were a wonderful granddaughter, and you brought great joy to his life. When you were born and he came to see you, I had to practically pry you off him. He sat with you in that big ugly rocking recliner we used to have and talked to you and told you jokes and insisted that you understood every word he said. 'She likes me best,' he kept saying. I think it made Dad a little jealous."

Hannah smiled, looked up at me.

"And when he said, 'Drop me a line,' what he meant was, Keep in touch. Which you certainly did."

"One time when I was six I called him when you weren't even home."

"Did you? What did you talk about?"

"Hamsters. I wanted one, and you wouldn't get me one. He told me"—she covered her mouth, started to giggle—"I still remember, exactly. He said, 'Oh, no, you don't want one of them; they eat their young. You don't want to be watching mama hamster spreading mustard on her baby, do you?' It was *weird*! *Do* they eat their young?"

"I have heard they do, sometimes. See how wise I was not to let you have one?"

Hannah shrugged. "I don't know. But anyway. I guess it's good he died right away, right?"

"Yes, for his sake."

"I wonder if he knew he was dying."

"I don't know, honey." I looked around the crowded room: men talking to men, women talking to women, mostly. "Don't know."

"What will Grandma do now?"

I looked over at my mother, standing next to Elaine Pinkers, the young woman who lives next door. My mother was talking animatedly. She could have been the perfect hostess except that she looked . . . puzzled.

"I don't know what Grandma will do. We'll have to see." Condo, I was thinking. Don't all widows move to condos and make container gardens on their balconies? Go out to lunch with friends and bring home leftovers that they eat for dinner? I'd have to come back and help her move at some point. And I'd tell Steve he had to help—no bowing out of this one.

"Aunt Caroline was crying in the bathroom," Hannah said.

"Was she?"

"Uh-huh. I came in by accident, and she was sitting on the edge of the bathtub crying real hard."

"Well, I suppose we'll all be doing some of that. But it's okay to cry, right?"

"Right. Mom?"

"Yes?"

"Don't take this wrong, okay? But when will we be going home?"

"Don't take *this* wrong. But as soon as we possibly can."

AFTER EVERYONE LEFT AND MY MOTHER WENT TO BED, Pete and I took our walk. At a school playground a few blocks away, we sat on a bench holding hands, saying nothing. When I started to cry, he pulled me closer, kissed the top of my head. "I'm so sorry."

I nodded, gulped back sobs.

"You want to stay for a while? I can take the kids home, and you could stay and help her figure out what she's going to do."

"I want to go home, though."

"Well, that's what we'll do, then."

"But you're right, I should stay. And not just to help Mom. I need to help Caroline. She's—oh, Pete, she told me the most awful things."

I repeated everything Caroline had said and waited for his reaction. It was not what I had expected. He simply nodded. "Sounds like you do need to be here for a while."

"But . . . don't you find this incredible?"

"Do you believe her?"

"I'm trying to, but I don't know. I can't imagine that these things went on in the house I lived in. That neither Steve nor I knew anything about it. I know my mother's odd about some things. And she's narcissistic—although any woman as beautiful as she was has that problem, it seems to me. But I can't imagine her doing such things."

"Okay."

"What does that mean?"

He looked at me, said nothing.

"What do you mean, 'Okay'?"

"I guess I mean the truth could be either or in between. And that I know this is bad, but it's not as shocking to me as it is to you." He turned toward me. "You know, I never told you this; I never wanted to. But maybe I should."

I waited, then finally said, "What?"

"I just . . . I don't want it to change the way you feel about my family."

"*What*, Pete?"

He leaned back against the bench. "You know why I hate swearing so much?"

"No. Why do you?"

"Because when we were really young, my father used to . . . when my brother and I did something wrong, Subby used to take us out to the garage and yank our pants down and beat the hell out of us. And the whole time he did it, he'd be swearing; it was the only time I ever heard him swear. He did this for a few years, and then he stopped. He just stopped. I don't know why. I don't know if he came to his senses or got in trouble or got some help or what happened. He just stopped."

"Wait. What about that story you told me once? When he pretended to hit you?"

"That's true. That was after."

"So when he hit you those other times, your mother knew?"

"She knew."

"Well, this is just . . . I'm astonished! It doesn't fit with them."

"It doesn't fit with what you know. Knew."

I swallowed hard, said nothing. But then, "You know, Pete, my dad just died. Why did you tell me that? I don't have room for anything else. Why did you tell me that?"

He put his arms around me, spoke softly into my ear. "Because something is not everything. You know? And because nobody knows what goes on in other families, because families lie about themselves to other people. Not only to other people but to one another. And to themselves."

I pulled away from him. "We don't! Our family doesn't!"

"Well. Maybe to a lesser degree."

"What do you mean! What do we lie about in our family?"

"All right. I want to say two things. Three things. One, we don't any of us always say what we really feel, do we? Not Hannah, not Anthony, not you or me. And aren't we lying to each other in that way?

"Two, we're not finished with one another as a family, and I hope we never will be. But things will come up. We will disappoint each other, we might—things will come up, that's all. People living with people makes for conflict. The truth is, we're not such a peaceful species. But the good part about conflict is that if you get through it you're stronger.

"Now. Three. Your dad did just die. And I want to help you. I want to make things easier for you. So let's talk about how to do that. And Laura? Sweetheart? I love you."

I took his hand, stared out at the jungle gym, the boxes-within-boxes pattern of it. Because of the angle. If you looked at it one way, you didn't see them. If you looked another way, you did. "I love you too," I said. The words seemed so small, a cardboard shield.

We sat without talking for a long time, and then I said, "I want to go home tomorrow and get some things. I want my work. Then I'll come back here and sort this all out."

MAGGIE ONCE TOLD ME ABOUT A FRIEND OF HERS who was diagnosed with ovarian cancer. "She only went to the doctor because she was having diarrhea," Maggie said. "She thought it was from a trip she'd taken to Mexico. The doctor told her she had about six months to live, at the outside. She said at first it was like she was lying under a pile of bricks. For about a week, all she did was lie on the sofa and cry. But then she got up and got going again. About a month before she died, she told me that something really good had come of this diagnosis: It had forced a reconciliation between her and a daughter with whom she'd not spoken in years. She said if it hadn't been for the cancer, she might have died without ever saying anything she needed so much to say, without ever saying anything true. I told her, 'But you can't be saying it was worth it, to have gotten this!' And she said yes, that was what she was saying. I said, 'Well, I have to tell you, I find that hard to believe. Surely there's a way other than catastrophe to learn to speak the truth.' And she said, 'Maybe there is. But I would never have found it. In the end, what does it matter how you find the thing you need most? Or even when? Just so long as you find it, and you can die in peace.'" Maggie looked over at me, her eyes full of tears. "But it does matter when," she said, and I said I knew. And then Maggie suddenly reached over to hug me so fiercely it hurt. "We're so lucky," she said, and I nodded into her shoulder. "It's kind of scary to be so lucky," she said, and I nodded again. I knew exactly what she meant. Sometimes being lucky is only waiting for a fall.

# 14

IT WAS SUCH A DIFFERENT CAR RIDE, GOING BACK. NO
fighting in the backseat. Only a respectful silence, occasionally punctuated by a neutral observation or a request
to have the radio tuned to another station. I looked out the
window and thought about the three of us siblings lined up
on my parents' bed that morning, being offered various
things of my father's by my mother, she in her bright, brittle way pulling open his drawers, rummaging through his
closet. Her eyes shining with tears that she clearly wanted
not to acknowledge. I'd taken only his hankies, his initials
embroidered in navy blue in one corner. Steve had taken
his watch and his cuff links—Steve is the only man I know
who still wears cuff links—and his stamp collection. Caroline took a photo of him that was taken just before he
married my mother. He stood beside an old jalopy, his foot
up on the bumper, smiling broadly. Everything else that
my mother had offered—his sweaters, his pipes, a

bathrobe he'd never worn—we had refused. I think it was just too early. None of us kids had been ready to put the kind of seal on his death that taking his things would do.

Whereas Steve and Caroline had tiptoed around each other, not speaking, not even looking at each other, she and I had restored an uneasy truce before I left; I told her I would return within the week, and that I'd call her as soon as I arrived back at my mother's house. Now, only a few miles from home, I regretted having made that promise. I felt I needed more time to reclaim my own life.

When we pulled into the driveway, I saw Maggie out in her yard, two houses down. She waved, smiling, then walked over to us. "How was it?" she asked as I got out of the car. Then, her smile disappearing, she said, "Oh. Jeez. Bad trip, huh?"

Pete and the kids greeted Maggie and then headed into the house, leaving us alone. "My dad died," I said.

She stared at me for a moment, trying to understand. "Just . . . now? While you were there?"

I nodded.

"Oh, my God." She hugged me, then stepped back to search my face. "I'm so sorry. Doug said you'd called. But I didn't have your number to call you back."

"I wasn't calling about that. That was before he even . . . I was calling about something else." I looked at our house and saw Pete passing in front of the living room window. He'd be checking everything out, making sure nothing had happened in our absence. The kids were undoubtedly ensconced in their rooms, reconnecting to their real selves as opposed to the hampered individuals they became when they were constantly in the presence of parents and relatives. *Anthony lite,* my son called himself in such situations.

"We can talk later," Maggie said. "You need to go in?"

"Actually, I think I need to go out. Can you?"

"Let me just go and tell Doug, and then I'll meet you back here. I'll pick you up. Where do you want to go?"

"I don't know."

"Well, alcohol or sugar?"

"Salty alcohol."

"Goldie's?" we said together, because of their famous nachos and margaritas. And laughed. It was so good to laugh. I felt as though I too were reentering my legitimate self.

I went into the house to tell Pete I was going out with Maggie, and he told me there was a message on the machine. My mother. Saying that she'd like to come and stay with us for a while. She wanted to fly in the next day.

"No," I said.

"*No?* Well, what are you going to tell her?"

"I'm going to tell her no."

"Laura."

"I said I'd go there!"

"She wants to come here. Do you really—"

"I'm going out with Maggie. I'll call her when I come back." I looked at the pile of mail and newspapers on the kitchen table. Even this seemed insurmountable. "I just need to go out for a while, Pete."

I went upstairs to tell Hannah I was leaving. She was sitting on her bed, talking on the phone. "Hold on," she said, and looked at me expectantly.

"I'm going out for a bit with Maggie. Okay?"

"Yeah. Can I go out for dinner and shopping for school clothes with Gracie?"

I'd forgotten all about school. It started in three days. "Yes, that would be great, in fact. Dad will give you some money. But remember—"

"I know," she said, rolling her eyes. "Don't spend too much on one thing. And get things that mix and match."

"That's right."

Next I went to Anthony's door, knocked. Nothing. I knocked again, heard him say, "Come in."

He was on his bed, *Sports Illustrated* lying across his belly.

"I just wanted to tell you I'm going out, okay? Dad will take care of dinner."

"Yeah, okay." It was defensive, the way he said this.

"Something wrong, Anthony?"

"No!"

I moved over to his bed, sat beside him. "What's up?"

"Nothing, I just . . . I heard you in the kitchen, with Dad. About Grandma."

I tried to remember exactly what I'd said, how I'd said it. "Yeah?"

"I don't know, I just think it's kind of screwed up that you don't want her to come here. It's probably pretty hard for her to be in that house. Like, everywhere she looks, she sees Grandpa. Maybe she just needs to get away."

"Well, Anthony."

He waited.

"It's just that there are a lot of things . . . I mean, I said I'd go there and help her."

"But maybe she—"

"You know what, sweetheart? Maggie's waiting for me. I'll talk to you about this later. I appreciate that you're concerned for Grandma. I do. But I—"

"Go!" he said. "Who's stopping you?" He returned to his magazine. I stood there for a moment, then headed downstairs. What was in my head were Pete's words: *We don't any of us always say what we really feel, do we?* It occurred to me to go back upstairs and tell Anthony the truth. But I didn't know it yet.

* * *

GOLDIE'S WAS NOMINALLY HALF BAR, half restaurant. But you could sit at the bar and have everything on the dinner menu, and you could sit in the restaurant for drinks only. Frank, the owner, was an easygoing guy; everything was okay with him. He had a mixed menu, everything from enchiladas to tandoori chicken to pecan-crusted catfish. Normally, you have to be wary of restaurants like that because, when they don't specialize in anything, nothing is good. But at Goldie's, everything was delicious. Frank once explained to me that his wife, Goldie, who died suddenly at age thirty-three, "never met a cuisine she couldn't conquer." Dinner at their house had always been an adventure; Frank never knew what he'd be coming home to, and he liked that. He'd been a stockbroker before she died; afterward, he decided to open a restaurant in her honor. He knew nothing about the business except that people out to eat were looking for variety and a really good meal, and that was exactly what he provided. He was sixty-one now, a good-looking man with thick gray hair and a stunning physique—he worked out every day to compensate for what he drank every night. I suppose Frank is an alcoholic, but he's an elegant and a sympathetic one. He started drinking seriously only after Goldie died; she'd been everything to him. They never had children, so Frank has fashioned a family out of his customers. He makes it his business to know—at least by name—anyone who comes in more than once.

So it was that when Maggie and I walked in, Frank, seated at the bar, called out, "Hey, Laura! How was the fair?"

"Oh, it was great." I looked over at Maggie, and without saying anything she agreed with me. Now was not the time.

"Bar or restaurant?" Frank asked. Then, reaching into the menu bin, "Late lunch, early dinner, or just drinks?"

"Loaded nachos and margaritas in the restaurant?" I said.

"You got it." Frank threw the menus back in the bin and led us to the back area that served as the restaurant. It was five-thirty, and we were the only ones in the place. "Sit anywhere you want," Frank told us, "and I'll put the order in for you."

I sat at a corner table and folded my hands tightly together on the white tablecloth. "So."

"Did you bring Kleenex?" Maggie asked.

"For what?"

She reached in her purse, took out a pack of tissues. "Here."

"I'm not going to cry."

"Okay."

"I'm not!"

She put the Kleenex back in her purse. Then she leaned forward, smiled a small smile. "It was awfully sudden, wasn't it?"

"Yeah. Stroke. He was in the hospital for a little stroke. And then he had a big one."

A young waitress appeared, using both hands to balance the tray holding our drinks. "*Here* we go!" she said, her loud cheerfulness an attempt to compensate for her insecurity. As far as I was concerned, her tip had just gone up threefold. She very carefully set our drinks before us, the pink tip of her tongue peeking out of the corner of her mouth. "And!" She looked brightly at us. "Anything else?"

"We ordered nachos," Maggie said. "Loaded."

"Uh-huh, Frank told me. But . . . anything else?"

"We're fine for now," I said. "We'll let you know if we need anything more."

"Okay. Oh! My name's Paula? And I'll be your server?"

"Okay, Paula."

I needed to make a suggestion for Frank's COMMENTS box. *Hey, Frank. Please be the only restaurant left that does not encourage your waitstaff to form intimate relationships with the customer.*

"So he died instantly, huh?" Maggie said. "I guess that's good. That's how my dad died too—a stroke. Only he didn't die right away, he was in a coma for a couple of days. It gave me some time to say some things. Sort of. I mean, I sat by his bed and said some things. And then—well, this is sort of embarrassing to admit—I was trying to be all New Age, and I said, 'It's okay, Daddy. You can go. Just go toward the light.' And my mom leaped out of her chair and rushed over and said, 'Oh, no, Tom, don't go! Don't leave me!' And she grabbed hold of him and started sobbing, and I stood there feeling just terrible."

I held up my glass, clinked it with Maggie's in an ironic toast, and had a long sip. "So what did you tell him?"

"My dad?"

"Yeah."

She looked away, watching Frank put a couple of tables together so he could seat a large group of people who had just come in. "I told him—oh, you know—thank you for helping me sell Girl Scout cookies door to door, for trying to teach me to catch a football, for telling me I was the prettiest girl in the yearbook when we both knew I wasn't. And I told him I loved him, you know, that I'd always . . . that he'd always be—" Our eyes filled with tears, and she dug in her purse to get us each a tissue. "Nothing covers it. No matter what you say. So don't feel bad that you didn't get a chance."

"But I do feel bad. I really do." I wiped at my eyes again.

"This will take some time, sweetheart. There's always going to be an ache. Our dads are—"

"I know." I started crying harder, making noise now, and looked at Maggie, panicked.

"You want me to quick change the subject?"

I nodded.

"Okay. Okay." She stood up, turned her back to me, and said over her shoulder, "Does my ass look like two watermelons in these pants?"

I blew my nose. "Yes."

"No, no, don't hold back, just tell me the truth."

She sat down, laughing, and we accepted the nachos our new friend Paula had brought over. I ate one, two, and then looked around the room, trying to steady myself. "Before my dad died, my sister Caroline told me some things about my mother."

"Okay, but first: *Does* my ass look like two watermelons?"

"No. . . . *Hams,* maybe."

"Oh, I see. Thanks a lot. I feel much better now. So. What things?"

I took another drink and began.


MUCH LATER, MAGGIE AND I were sitting in the bleachers of the high school football stadium, where we'd come to talk after Goldie's closed. The stars were so clear; constellations stood out as plainly as star maps. I squinted at my watch. "Whoa, it's two-thirty!"

"Will Pete worry?"

"No. He'll go to bed. How about Doug?"

"He'll worry a little, but that's all right."

I stood, a bit unsteady. I didn't know how much I'd drunk, but it was much more than usual. "We should go."

She took hold of my hand, pulled me down. "In a minute. I want to tell you something first."

"What?"

"Just this story, about . . . well, I used to stay with an aunt and uncle every summer. My family would go to visit them because they lived on a lake—in fact, the whole extended family would come up and find cottages and use their house as headquarters. But I stayed in the house. They had a daughter my age, and I slept on a cot in her room. I loved that family, especially my Uncle Harold. He was hand-some, and funny, and so kind. But one summer when I was nine, he spanked me—grabbed me by the arm and swatted me maybe five, six times. He did it in front of other people, I remember; that was one of the worst things, it was so embarrassing. We were in the hallway, but there were a bunch of relatives in the living room who could see us. The front door was open; it was a beautiful day. I remember a breeze that smelled like water, I remember the cotton ball they had bobby-pinned on the screen to keep the flies away, I remember the red shorts I was wearing with this striped shirt with spaghetti straps that tied over my shoulders and the straps hurt that day because I was sun-burned. I remember all that. But I don't know why he spanked me, I cannot for the life of me remember why. It was just that one time, but it devastated me. I never wanted to stay with them again. I felt afraid of him; I just saw him as a completely different person."

"Meaning what? That Caroline suffered one little thing and blew it all out of proportion?"

"Well . . . is it possible? Does it make sense to you that that might have happened? Perhaps . . . a few times?"

"I don't know. Maybe."

"I mean, I never changed my mind about that uncle. Even now when I see him I feel a little afraid. And he's just this little stooped-over gray-haired guy. Last year, at a family picnic, I was sitting by him and I all of a sudden said, 'Do you remember the time you spanked me?' And he said, 'No. When did I do that?' And I knew he really didn't remember, and there was no point in bringing it up. I don't know why I *did* bring it up."

"You probably wanted him to apologize."

"I don't think it was that, really. I think I wanted to stop being afraid of him. You know?"

"Oh, Maggie. What should I do? If I let my mother come and stay with me, I betray Caroline. If I tell Mom not to, I betray her at a time when she's really hurting."

"Tell her to come," Maggie said. "Let her be with your family. Then you go and see Caroline. Let her finish."

I sighed deeply.

"Just an idea."

"It's a good idea. I could get together with Caroline and Steve—he's still in town, visiting some of his old high school friends. Maybe if she can just finish saying all she wanted to say, if we can both say we *support* her." I rolled my eyes.

"Would Steve come?"

"Yeah, I think he would. For a few hours or so, anyway. He would if I asked him. I could tell him he needs to come and help Caroline and me do things in the house. Then we could kind of ease into it. I think it's important that Caroline talk to him too."

"I'll cover for you with the kids. Tell them to come over if they need anything. I can work from home better than I can work in the office, anyway. I only go to the office for the doughnuts."

I kissed her forehead. "Oh, Maggie. Thank you. What would I do without you?"

"Let's go home," Maggie said. "You're getting a little sentimental here."

We walked across the field with our arms linked. The only sound was our footsteps, walking over grass grown stiff and strawlike in the absence of rain. I watched the fireflies, their little lights appearing, disappearing, appearing, disappearing.

WHEN I SLID INTO BED BESIDE PETE, I had not exfoliated or washed or toned my face. I had not flossed or brushed my teeth or shoved the proxi-brush between them, or rubber-tipped my gums or scraped my tongue. I had not put on my five-billion-dollar-an-ounce moisturizer that undoubtedly did nothing that Vaseline couldn't. I had not delicately pulled up the flab on my neck and then looked at myself from various angles, sadly considering plastic surgery. I had not taken my gingko biloba in an effort to help my failing memory. A friend of mine recently said about gingko biloba, "I think whatever-that-stuff-is-called works great. I just keep forgetting to take it." Another friend told me about a time she'd answered her cell phone and told her girlfriend, who was the caller, that she was in the parking lot of her doctor's office, getting ready to go in for an appointment, but she was early; she had some time to talk. They chatted for a while and then the woman happened to look down into her purse at the empty carrier for her cell phone. She told her friend, "Dammit, I lost my cell phone." Wait. It gets worse. The friend says, "Well, let's retrace your steps."

So I had not done any of my usual nightly routine and it felt wonderful. I wondered why I cluttered my life so much. I felt so free: I had bothered only to remove my sandals and my pants and to lie down on what was approximately my side of the bed—which felt suddenly like a boat on an angry sea. I put one foot on the floor, and things stopped moving.

"What time is it?" Pete asked.

I looked at the bedside clock and then spoke with great precision—as well as good cheer, I thought; I sounded really very cheerful. "One after three!"

Pete raised himself up on one elbow and looked over at me. "Oh, boy, you're in great shape. Maggie drove, right?"

"Yesh." The roof of my mouth was numb. I touched my lips experimentally. Some feeling there. The face of my dentist, Dr. Paine (I know; he knows; we all know) appeared in my head, his green goggles and paper mask, his curly black hair. *Numb yet, Laura?* No. Not yet.

"Did Maggie drink as much as—"

"No! Jesus—oops! Sorry."

He turned on his bedside lamp.

I shaded my eyes, squinted at him. "What. Are you mad?"

"No. I think you deserved a night out." He turned out the light again.

"Pete?"

"Yeah."

"Tell me a memory."

"I'm tired, Laura. Come on."

"I need to, though. I mean, I need you to." I turned to face him, felt dizzy, and turned back. "I'll tell *you* one."

Nothing. But he hadn't gone back to sleep; I could tell from his breathing.

"Once I got sent to the principal's office for making fun of the math teacher's chin. Which was this huge double chin, like a purse. Mrs. Menafee. Your turn."

Pete groaned. "I don't have one, Laura."

"Yes, you do. Tell me. We've never missed a night, Pete."

He turned on the light again. "Are you all right?"

I shaded my eyes with the pillow. "Yesh."

He gently pulled the pillow away from me. He was wide awake now. "Did you tell Maggie? About Caroline?"

"Uh-huh. We talked about it for a long time. A looooooong time."

"What did she say?"

I took back the pillow, covered my eyes again. "Turn off the light, okay?"

I heard the click of the switch, and then Pete said, again, "What did she say?"

Suddenly, my spirits fell and I was exhausted. I plumped the pillow, arranged it carefully under my head. "She has an idea. I want to talk to you about it. But tomorrow. Tell me a memory and let's go to sleep. A short memory. Not sad."

He lay flat, thought for a moment, and then said, "Okay. Once, I ran away. And the only thing in my suitcase was salami sandwiches."

"How old were you?"

"Eighteen."

I giggled. "Come on."

"I'm serious. I thought I'd figure out the rest later. I was walking to the bus station when Subby found me."

"What did he do?"

"We went to a park and ate some sandwiches and then he took me home."

"What did Rosa do?"

"Smacked me on the back of the head and then hugged me and then made me something to eat."

I thought of Rosa in her apron, weak in the knees with relief, hitting the head of the son she was so happy to see. I wondered how often it was transmogrified love that made for the worst lashings-out. Something needled at me, making me wake up a little more. "How were the kids tonight?"

"I hardly saw Hannah. She came back with some clothes. And some hair . . . semen."

"What?"

"Well, that's what it looks like. You know, gel, whatever. Hair goop."

"Hmm. She's getting more and more interested in the way she looks. What style clothes did she get?"

"I don't know—she'll show you tomorrow. Anthony and I went and got steaks at McMannus's."

"How was he?"

"Anthony? Fine. Why?"

"Was he mad at me?"

"No. Why?"

"He thinks my mother should come and stay here."

Silence.

"Pete?"

"Yeah?"

"You do too?"

"Go to sleep, Laura. We'll talk tomorrow."

"Okay, but my today thing? Maggie wants another baby."

"Are you serious?"

"She isn't going to, she just *wants* one."

"Oh. Well, me too. That's my today thing. Okay? Good night."

"You want another baby?" I saw myself in a rocking chair, looking down at my new baby. With my old neck. "You want a *baby*?"

"Sure. But not really."

I lay still for a while, then said, "I'm so glad to be home."

Nothing.

"Pete?"

A deep snore. I closed my eyes and hoped I could sleep late.


IT WAS NOT TO BE. At a little before five, I heard Hannah in the bathroom, moaning. I got out of bed and found her sitting doubled over on the edge of the tub. I knelt down beside her. "Hannah? What's wrong?"

She pushed her hair out of her eyes, looked up at me, and her expression instantly changed. "What happened to you?"

"What do you mean?"

"What *happened* to you?"

"Nothing."

"You look . . . look how you look!"

I went to the mirror, turned quickly away. Then I knelt beside Hannah again. "I'm just . . . I didn't wash my face last night."

She stared at me, considering. Then she said, "I have cramps so bad. Why do we have to get cramps on top of having to have stupid periods?"

"I don't know. Maybe to practice for childbirth."

"And *that* hurts way more than this!"

"You forget all about it, though," I said, perpetuating the lie in the time-honored tradition. I went over to the medicine chest and opened it, surveyed the contents.

"I just did."

"What?"

"I just took something."

"What did you take?"

"Advil."

"Okay. So, go on back to bed. I'll get the heating pad for you. I'll lie down with you."

She headed out of the bathroom, saying over her shoulder, "Mom? No offense, but could you, like, brush your teeth?"

I brushed my teeth, washed my face, took a couple of Advil myself, and then went to the linen closet for the heating pad. This is a sign, I was thinking. I can't go anywhere. My kids need me. This is a clear message: You're needed here more than there.

I plugged in the heating pad, gave it to Hannah, and lay down beside her. "Poor baby."

"What?" Her voice was muffled, miserable—her head was buried under her pillow.

"I said, 'Poor baby.' Ish a drag, huh?"

She lifted her pillow, looked over at me. "Are you drunk?"

I said nothing.

"Mom! Are you *drunk*?"

"Oh, not so much."

"I can't believe you're drunk! Gross!"

I sobered up to the best of my ability, concentrated mightily on my articulation. "I had too much to drink. That is true. But I am here to offer you comfort nonetheless. I know how much it can hurt when you get bad cramps."

She lay back down. I was marginally forgiven. "Yeah. What do boys get? They don't get *anything*."

"Oh, of course they do."

"What?"

"They get . . . blamed for the sins of their fathers."

"What do you mean?"

"People still call men pigs, even though they're so much better than they used to be. You know. Think how it would feel to be called that."

She considered this. "It's better than cramps. I really get them bad, Mom."

"I know, sweetheart. I used to, too. Once, when I was your age, I got them in school and I took some Midol that a friend gave me. And I think I took too many or something, because I really flipped out."

"Why? What happened?"

"I don't know. I just got . . . weird. I went in the bathroom and was sitting on the floor—I remember I was wearing my Girls' Madrigals uniform, this awful green jumper, because we had a performance that afternoon. Anyway, I was sitting there and I was really hurting and someone went and got the nurse and I just went *nuts* on her. I was awful . . . wouldn't tell her my name, wouldn't let her help me."

"Why?" Hannah leaned up on an elbow, stared intently at me.

"I honestly don't know."

"So what happened?"

"The principal came. Then the nurse called my mother and told her I was not cooperating with her, I was behaving very oddly, and I had mistreated her, and Grandma came and got me."

"Was she mad?"

"No, she wasn't mad." I remembered her driving me home, silent. Not in anger but in a kind of complicity—she'd reached over and touched my knee, smiled. Tucked me in my bed when I got home, brought me a heating pad and a drink of blackberry brandy, which was her cure for cramps.

Hannah lay flat, the heels of her hands pushing against the heating pad. I used to do that too—as though it would push the heat through to displace the pain. "That's bizarre that you did that," she said, yawning.

"I know."

"Why'd you tell me that story?"

I laughed. "I don't know. I just remembered it."

"Okay, I'm going back to sleep. Don't wake me up even if I sleep till noon." She turned away from me.

I pulled the covers up over her shoulder. Then I lay back down and stared at the ceiling, too awake now to sleep any longer.

*It is Steve and me, sitting cross-legged on the living room floor on a sunny afternoon, our heads bent together over a game of Monopoly. We are about six and ten, happily engrossed, both of us smiling, he because he's learning a "big kid" game, me because I am winning, no doubt—I almost never lost at Monopoly, no matter who I played. In the background, Caroline lies on the sofa in her pajamas. She has the chicken pox. She is clutching her big yellow teddy bear to her breast, craning her neck to try to see the game board. I remember that Caroline named the bear Hope, and we all thought it was so weird. Hope has the chicken pox too: red construction-paper dots, which Caroline carefully cut out and Scotch-taped onto him. While Steve and I sit playing the game with our backs to her, she takes what consolation she can from something she created. I remember her telling my mother that day that her throat hurt, the chicken pox were in her throat, and my mother telling her not to be ridiculous. Years later, when Hannah got chicken pox and I took her to the pediatrician, he looked in her throat and said, "Yup."*

# 15

"YOU DON'T HAVE TO DRIVE," I TOLD MY MOTHER. "It's fine for you to fly. You won't need a car here. You don't like to drive long distances. You don't like to drive *short* distances!" Silently, I added, *And I am not going to come and get you and bring you here.*

"But I'll be there for a whole week," she said. "And you'll be working, and the kids are going to go back to school. . . . What if I want to go out somewhere? I don't want to leave you without a car."

"You can take it anytime. I don't really use it that much." I didn't want to tell her I was going to her house the day after she arrived here.

It was a rainy Monday morning. Just before I called my mother, I spoke to Caroline and Steve, both of whom agreed to meet me at our mother's house on Wednesday afternoon, presumably to talk about what to do with the place—Mom had always said she wouldn't want to live there alone. Whether she still felt that way, I didn't know, but I wasn't going to ask now. Steve had been a little put out. I'd awakened him from a sound sleep, and he had been intending to go home today. But he agreed, finally, after I convinced him he might as well take care of this now instead of having to fly back later. He had also agreed to pick me up at the airport. That way I could work on him a bit before he saw Caroline.

Thunder boomed so loudly I could feel it in my chest. The rain, coming in at an angle, fell in sheets against the windows. I couldn't believe the storm hadn't awakened the kids. I wanted to get off the phone—I'd heard you shouldn't use portables in such weather. I got a brief little vision of a cartoon death, a jagged bolt of lightning coming from the phone into my brain, my hair standing on end, my eyes turned spirally, and the toes of my shoes curled up. "I've got to go, Mom," I said. "I'll see you tomorrow."

I hung up the phone, went over to the coffeemaker to fill my mug, and sat at the table with Pete. "Here we go."

He looked up at me briefly and returned to the business section of the newspaper.

"I feel bad leaving when school's just starting."

"They'll be fine," Pete said. "They don't need us anymore."

"Yes, they do!"

"Not that way. Anyway, I'll be here. And Maggie always helps."

I reached for the front section of the paper, scanned the headlines. "Why don't they ever lead with good news?"

"Because people pay more attention to bad news."

"No, they don't. That's what you always say. It isn't true!"

He put down the newspaper. "You want to fight, Laura? Do you need to fight?"

I said nothing, blinked once, twice.

"What are you so mad about?"

"I'm not." I started reading the paper, then stopped. "I'm *not*. I just . . . don't want to do this. I want to stay home and work. I've got work to do. A family to care for. I want to live my own life, not try to straighten out someone else's."

"She's your sister!"

"I don't even know what that means."

He stared at me, half smiling, *Are you kidding?*

"Well, I *don't* know. She wasn't normal. We didn't have a sisterly relationship, you know that. She . . . come on, this is a kid who used to tell me she could talk to dead people, okay? Not for creepy fun. She meant it."

Pete walked over to the sink, rinsed out his cup, and put it in the dishwasher. Pointedly remained silent.

"What?" I said, my back to him.

"Nothing."

I turned around. "Pete. What?"

"If it were Maggie having trouble . . ."

"Yeah? What, would I go out of my way to help her? Of course! But you know what? I don't know if I buy into the *It's your family, you've got to* thing. Maybe sometimes you make a family out of other people."

Pete came over to the table and sat down again. "You may have more in common with other people, Laura. But you have your bio-logical family for life, right or wrong."

"Well, I know that. But does that mean——?"

"Yes." He looked at his watch and got up. "I've got to go. I'll see you tonight."

"Wait!"

He turned around, a little impatient, I saw, so I said, "Never mind." I stood at the window to watch him drive away and then I went upstairs to shower. After that, I'd go into the basement, to my sewing room, to think about color and texture and patterns that have nothing to do with personalities. Only, of course they do. I remember Anthony once asking me, when he was maybe six, "If you could understand *everything* about just one thing, wouldn't you understand everything about everything? Because of how everything is all tied up together? And that's why nobody understands anything all the way except God?"

I TURNED ON THE FLUORESCENT OVERHEAD in my studio and looked around. What anticipatory pleasure I was enjoying already! There was my machine, recently cleaned and oiled and ready to go, all but transforming itself now into a metallic beckoning finger. There were my rotary cutters, lined up in order of size. There was the wooden multitiered riser holding all my spools of thread, over a hundred different colors, organized by hue and by type: cottons, metallics, silks, polyesters, quilting threads. I had drawers full of various notions: needles, thimbles, straight and safety pins, snaps in every size, tape measures and rulers, thin slivers of soap that I used to mark quilts, embroidery scissors, six- and eight- and ten-inch shears, a heavy silver pair of pinking shears, seam bindings and seam rippers, yards of elastics and Velcro. I had shelves of books on textiles, on buttons, on patterns, on every kind of quilt from antique Amish to contemporary, on hand and machine and sashiko quilting techniques. I even had volumes of poetry I read sometimes for a kind of oblique inspiration. I had patterns of my own design cut from sandpaper and stored carefully away in manila envelopes, endless varieties of beads and sequins, yarns and embroidery floss, fabric paint, tassels, and trims. I had graph paper and plastic templates in the shape of squares, triangles, and half circles.

And fabric! Big square wicker baskets lined up on deep wall shelves and full of solid or printed cottons, silks, batiks, woolens, blends—you name it, I had some. One of the many reasons I liked to be in fabric stores was that I was surrounded by people who shared the same benign illness as I. Once, waiting in line to pay for a nice selection of miniature florals, I'd heard the woman ahead of me say, "I have to hurry up and get home and hide this. If my husband sees me bringing in more fabric, he'll kill me." "Oh, I know," the woman she'd spoken to had answered. "I've been hiding mine for years. Try taking it home in a grocery bag. Just throw a box of Kotex on top and he won't go near it." That second woman had such a high pile of fabric in her arms she could hardly see over it. When the clerk who rang her up had asked what she was going to make with it, the woman answered with no sense of irony whatsoever, "Nothing." I smiled at the woman behind me, who shrugged and said, "You know what they say. Whoever dies with the most fabric wins."

Sometimes, a dinner guest will ask to see my studio—it's almost always a woman, although occasionally a man will want to see—and whenever they do, they stand still in appreciative wonder (the men with their hands in their pockets) and usually say just one word: *Wow*. It doesn't matter if they like to sew or not, they just appreciate seeing a room so completely stocked, so richly reflective of a person's passion. It's similar to the way a lot of people love hardware stores. Whether you know what the things are or not, they're *all there*.

On the flannel display board, a few vintage hankies were positioned *en pointe*, a suggestion for a quilt to be made from them. I'd been collecting these hankies for years. Such dainty imprints of social history were recorded there: florals from the twenties and thirties, Mr. and Mrs. hankies from the forties, whimsical patterns of floating toasters and Scottie dogs from the fifties. There were leaf designs for fall, reindeer and candy canes for Christmas, flocked velvet hearts for Valentine's Day, white-on-white embroidery with wide lace trim for weddings. One dark-red hankie had *Lipstick* embroidered on one corner. An ancient pale-blue one with an embroidered nosegay of violets was my favorite—I doubted I'd ever do anything but look at it. All the hankies were worn to a powderlike softness from washing, ironing, folding, holding; from tears. Sometimes I put the old hatbox I kept them in on my lap and just slowly sifted though them, looking to feel memories.

I was anxious to begin that hankie quilt, but first I needed to finish the one I'd been commissioned to do. I'd get the borders on, sew a scattering of seed pearls across it, and back, bind, and machine-quilt it today. Tomorrow morning, on the way to pick up my mother at the airport, I would mail it in the usual way, wrapped in a silk-lined storage bag made out of scraps of fabric that were used in the quilt. Customers went crazy for those bags. Some, it was the reflexive pleasure of receiving an unexpected gift. But I thought maybe it was also because we've become so unused to people doing anything beyond what they're paid to do.

The phone rang. I let it ring a few more times, thinking it was Pete calling to say he was sorry for having been so gruff, and wanting to punish him a little in this passive-aggressive way. But it was not Pete, it was Karen Benson, with whom I had made an appointment for today and about which I had forgotten completely. She was calling to say she was going to be about forty-five minutes late; was that okay? "Oh, don't worry," I said. "I'll just be here, working." After I hung up, I looked at my calendar to see what kind of quilt she had called about. I found her name next to the time she was to arrive—ten minutes from now—and beneath that I saw a note for what she wanted done: a dog quilt. For a dog? I wondered. In honor of a dog? Using dog-motif fabrics? I needed to be more thorough about taking information when I made appointments. For one thing, I liked to lay out samples of materials before people arrived.

I got out my basket of flannels, pulled some green and brown plaids, and then went through the novelty prints in case she was a literal kind of customer. I had a cotton print that was nothing but goofy-looking cartoon dogs and one slightly more elegant one featuring hunting dogs. I was digging through my solids when I heard the back door open and Maggie calling my name.

"Down here!" I called back, and smiled at her when she came into the studio. "Hey."

"Guess what I have." She held out a bakery bag.

"Oh, God, Maggie, I just came back from the fair. And from a funeral, where you eat even more. Because . . . you know, you can."

"I only got two. And they're fat free!"

"Really?" I asked, looking in the bag.

"No. But I think if you tell yourself it is, your body processes it that way."

"No, thanks, Maggie."

She sat in my chair and started eating a Bismarck. "I just got in kind of a fight at the grocery store."

"Why? What happened?"

"Okay. I'm looking for Bisquick Light, right? For this recipe I found for chicken and dumplings? And I ask the stock guy do they have it. He's not sure. And then he says, in this really snotty tone of voice, 'I don't need that stuff to make pancakes.' I say, 'Well, I don't either.' He says, 'So why do you want it?'

"I'm thinking, *What is this?* and I say, 'That is none of your business!' He takes a look on the shelf and says, 'There isn't any. We're out of it. I guess *nobody* can figure out how to make pancakes,' and he walks off down the aisle. I yell after him, 'Hey! I make my pancakes from *scratch*! With *buttermilk*!' So here's my question: Am I cracking up?"

"I have Bisquick Light," I said, laying a solid tan flannel next to a green-and-black mini-check.

"Good. But am I? Cracking up?"

I stopped digging through fabric to look at her. "No. You just care too much about what other people think. That's a problem most of us have."

"I suppose." She licked off her fingers, then came to stand beside me. "What are you making?"

"I'm not sure yet. A client I'm meeting with wants a quilt having something to do with dogs."

"Hmmm. That could be fun."

"Yeah, it could."

"You could sew on real dog toys. Little squeaky ones."

I pulled out my gigantic clear-plastic box of buttons and handed it to her. "Look through here for anything having to do with dogs. In any way."

She rifled through the buttons while I looked at a few more fabrics, then said, "Voilà!"

I turned around.

"You have buttons with paw prints!"

"Well, see?" I said. "That's why I always buy anything that strikes my fancy. Whatever I get, I'll end up using eventually. Pull them out. I'll take them with me to Minnesota."

"So you're going, huh?"

"Yeah. I followed your advice. My mother's coming here tomorrow. Then the next day, I'll go there and meet with Steve and Caroline."

"Good."

"I guess. But I have to tell you, I wish I didn't have to do it."

"I know. But you do have to."

"I'm just too *busy.*"

Maggie scrunched up the bakery bag, tossed it in the trash.

"You ate *both?*"

She shrugged. "It's your fault."

"Right."

"I want to ask you something, Laura. Don't take this the wrong way. But do you think the reason you don't want to go is because you're afraid you'll find out something you don't want to admit about yourself?"

"Oh, man."

"Okay, forget it. I dreamed I was Jenny Jones in my Maidenform bra. Sorry."

"No, *I'm* sorry. I guess there might be some truth to that; that's why I'm so jumpy about it. It's pretty awful to think you let someone suffer and did nothing about it. Kept yourself oblivious. I read this story once about a girl who watched a bully beat up another girl. She was in a ring of kids, all of them just watching the blood, the snot—it was kind of an awful thing to read. I remember thinking, I'd never do that, I'd never just watch. Easy to make yourself a hero in the abstract, huh?"

Maggie shrugged. "Well, it's also hard to leap in when there's a chance it will make the bully turn on you. And anyway, maybe you didn't keep yourself oblivious. Maybe you truly were unaware."

I started pulling out pieces of fabric. A nice red. A sunny yellow. Strong colors. Primary. Clear.

"You could put dog tags on that quilt too," Maggie said. "You can get them made at Petco—you engrave them yourself. You could get *Fido* and *Rex*. And *Spot*.

"That's a good idea. Can I steal it?"

"Of course. For five bucks."

I put down the fabric. "Come upstairs with me."

"Laura! You don't have to pay me! I was kidding!"

"I know. I'm going to give you the Bisquick and kick you out. I have to work."

"Me too. I'm working from home."

"Yes. I can see that."

When we were in the kitchen, Maggie saw a book I'd just finished lying on the kitchen table. She picked it up, leafed through it, then checked the spine. "*Lost Lake*. Mark Slouka. Is he any good?"

"It's actually one of the best books I've read."

"Can I borrow it?"

"Sure."

"Okay, I'll see you later then. Come over when you're finished working." I closed the door after her, started for my studio, and turned around when I heard Maggie come back in. "Bisquick," she said.

I was halfway down the stairs when I heard Anthony. "Mom? Are you making breakfast? Will you?"

Someday, I would miss this, I knew.

*It is a photo taken at Christmastime, a picture of our tree. I look at how beautifully decorated it is, and I remember how the tinsel was painstakingly hung by my mother, one long strand at a time, so that the tree shimmered. Some ornaments are store-bought but many are homemade. I see a Santa I made from a lightbulb, an angel I made from a doily, a snowman out of cotton balls. There is a pair of felt mittens attached to each other by red yarn that Steve made in kinder-garten and sprinkled liberally with glitter, and there are the red and green paper chains he loved to make because he got to use the stapler. There is a gingerbread man he made from Play-Doh. You can't see anything Caroline made because her things hang in the back. I told her to put them there be-cause the tree was stationed in front of a window, and I said if she put them on the back, everyone would see her things first. Everyone outside. Years later, I told someone this, and we both laughed. It seemed funny then, just a little* Father Knows Best *type of sibling upsmanship. I see it differently now. Which is to say, I see it.*

# 16

"SO HOW ARE YOU, MOM?" I SAID, AS WE PULLED AWAY
from the airport.

I hardly needed to ask. She looked awful: puffy bags
under her eyes, her hair disheveled, her outfit appropriate
for anyone else but alarming for my mother: a lightweight
gray sweatsuit and sneakers.

She leaned back in her seat and sighed. Looked out the
window. "As well as can be expected, I suppose. Such a
shock. And you know, Laura, I think I see him *everywhere*.
I mean that literally."

I looked quickly over at her. "You mean you're hallu-
cinating?"

"No, it's . . . well, on the airporter, for example, I saw a
man in the front of the bus, and it looked exactly like your
father. Exactly. I stared at him the whole way. I thought
about going up to him, but what would I have said? *Oh,
Stan, is it you?* I see him walking down the sidewalk, in

stores at the mall, even in the house—I come into a room and see him slip around the corner. Just . . . *zip!*" She laughed, a small sound.

I nodded, said nothing.

"Is that happening to you too?"

"No, but I've heard about it happening to other people. To other widows."

"Oh? And what else have you heard?"

"About widows?"

"Yes."

I pulled up at a stop sign, reached over to touch her shoulder. "Whatever you're feeling, it's normal. That's what I've heard."

"Well."

I started driving again, then said in as innocuous a way as I could, "You know, Mom, I was thinking I'd go back to Minnesota. I want to see Caroline again. And Steve, before he goes back home."

"What? Well, why didn't—"

"I mean see them alone. Just some brother-and-sister time, without anyone else. Some time to talk. You know? When we were there, we didn't really get . . . well, you know, Dad died and . . ." It still felt strange to say it. I had an impulse to say, *Sorry, Dad,* as though this were some tasteless joke we were all playing on one another.

My mother stared straight ahead, eyebrows raised just the slightest bit.

"The truth is, Caroline's having some trouble, and—"

"Your sister is *always* having trouble. Always. It is the way she prefers to live."

I pulled up to a red light, looked over at her. "Yeah. Did you ever wonder about why?"

"She is that type of personality. She just is. You can let it drive you crazy, or you can just let her be. Green light." She reached in her purse and pulled out a Kleenex. Wiped at her nose. "Can we talk about something else?"

"Sure. Of course. Oh, listen, you'll love this. Hannah went out to buy some clothes the other day, for school? She came back with—"

"I don't see why you have to go back there when I just arrived! Why can't you just stay here while I'm here and then we can go back together?"

I hesitated, then said, "Mom, I'm sorry this is upsetting to you. It's just something I have to do. Maybe I shouldn't have told you now, when you just got here. I guess I wanted to get it out of the way. Let's have a nice dinner tonight." I smiled over at her. "Okay? I'm glad you're here, Mom. Everyone's glad."

She closed her eyes briefly, opened them. "Maybe I should go back home. I don't know what to do."

I signaled for my exit off the freeway. "Almost there," I said. I meant it to be reassuring, even gay. It was neither.

JUST BEFORE I WAS READY TO PUT DINNER on the table, the phone rang. It was Aunt Fran. "Hey, how are you?" I asked her.

"Oh, the same as always. Rich and famous. And you?"

"Just getting dinner. We're having your recipe for cucumber salad."

"Well, listen, can I talk to your mom quickly? She called and left a message earlier."

"Oh! Sure." *When? What message?*

I went to the foot of the stairs and called up to my mother. She had spent some time in the guest room after she arrived, then came down in a better mood to help me make dinner. Now she was up in Hannah's room, going over her wardrobe with her.

"Aunt Fran's on the phone," I yelled. She answered that she'd take it in the guest room.

"Dinner's just about ready," I said.

Nothing.

"Mom?"

"Go ahead and get started; I'll be right down."

I went back into the kitchen, picked up the phone, heard my mother say breathlessly, "So I need you to—" and then, "Laura?" I hung up, flipped the turkey burgers for the last time, dumped the oven-baked French fries into a basket and salted them, sliced tomatoes, drained the water off the ears of corn, yelled up for Anthony and Hannah, and then went to the basement door to call Pete up out of his workroom. I once read an essay about a woman used to a large family making dinner for only herself, the oddity and awful stillness of it. I can imagine. There are random moments—tossing a salad, coming up the driveway to the house, ironing the seams flat on a quilt square, standing at the kitchen window and looking out at the delphiniums, hearing a burst of laughter from one of my children's rooms—when I feel a wavelike rush of joy. This is my true religion: arbitrary moments of nearly painful happiness for a life I feel privileged to lead. Think of the way you sometimes see a tiny shaft of sunlight burst through a gap between rocks, the way it then expands to illuminate a much larger space—it's like that. And it's like quilting, a thread surfacing and then disappearing into the fabric of ordinary days. It's not always visible, but it's what holds everything together.

"SO YOU'LL BE AT THE HOUSE in a little over two hours?" my mother asked.

"Closer to three, probably." I turned around to look at her in the backseat. She'd come along with Pete to drop me off at the airport. "You know that, right? Why are you asking?"

"No reason. I guess I'm old enough that I'm still in awe of how quickly you can get somewhere."

"I guess I'm old, then," Pete said. "I'm amazed too."

"Wait until your *children* get old," my mother said. "Then you'll know what old is!"

I straightened in my seat. "I'm not old!"

"That's not what you tell me," Pete said.

I gave him a look, then pointed at the United sign up ahead.

"I see it," he said. "Now let's see if they'll actually let me stop long enough to let you out." He pulled up to the curb and I grabbed my suitcase, gave Pete a quick kiss, and then pecked my mother's cheek as she came out of the backseat to get into the front. "Say hello to Steve for me," she said.

"I will." And Caroline?

No message for her, apparently, unless it was in the way my mother slammed the car door. She waved, and then she and Pete drove off. I watched them go, wanting to go back home with them. Instead, I wheeled my bag inside to check the flight information board. ON TIME, it said. This, I have learned, is like a serving suggestion: what you see wasn't necessarily what you get. ON TIME usually means they haven't announced the delay yet. I grieve for the airlines, and I hate them.

I stopped at a kiosk before I headed for the gate. This is my deal: If I have to fly, I get a *People* magazine and a giant-size Snickers. I tell myself it's so that if there's one of those interminable stuck-on-the-tarmac delays and everyone is starving, I can say, "I have a candy bar. I'll share." But the truth is, the one time I was on a flight where there was a terrible delay, I ate the whole thing myself—one small secret bite at a time. I never tasted anything more delicious. I think my seatmate smelled the peanuts on my breath when I ate it; she snuck envious little glances at me while I looked out the window at the unchanging view on the runway. Half of me said, Would it kill you to give her some? The other half said, Did she not pass the same kiosk as I?

# 17

STEVE WAS GOING TO BE A FEW MINUTES LATE PICKING me up because, unbelievably, the flight arrived more than half an hour early. I was sitting on a bench outside the airport, watching two young lovers kiss hello, when he pulled up and honked, then yelled my name.

"Sorry," I said, getting in the car. "I was distracted." I pointed to the rapturously kissing couple. "Are you and Tessa still like that?"

He looked at them in the rearview mirror. "Nah."

"How long were you like that?"

"I don't know; couple of hours."

I put on my seatbelt and pushed my hair back from my forehead. "How are you, sweetie?"

He shrugged. "I know what's up, in case you're wondering. There's no way in hell we'll be talking about what to do with the sideboard."

"Thanks for staying."

"I'm doing it for you, you know."

"And I'll bet Tessa asked you to."

Nothing.

"Didn't she?"

"Yeah, but I would have done it for you anyway."

"Uh-huh."

"I would! And anyway, what the hell, let Caroline get it out of her system. Whatever's *in* her system. Maybe then she'll stop her . . . stuff."

We rode in silence the rest of the way, but for the radio, the volume turned low. When we arrived, there was a car in the driveway. I wasn't sure, but I thought it was Aunt Fran's. Sure enough, when I stepped onto the porch and started to open the door, she opened it instead.

Her hand flew to her chest. "Oh! You're here!"

I laughed. "I was going to say the same thing! What are you doing?"

"I just came over to stock the fridge. You know how your mother is. God forbid you arrive and there's not enough to eat. I just put some things in there . . . a few things, you know, milk . . . So! How was the flight? Early, huh?"

"Yes," I said, thinking, *What is she so nervous about?* And then I realized my mother must have told her why we're here. Most sisters do talk, after all. That phone call last night. My mother must have told Aunt Fran about the Meeting.

Steve, after greeting Aunt Fran, disappeared into the den to check his messages. When he was through returning calls, we'd go to meet Caroline for an early dinner, then come back here for our talk.

"Call me if you need anything," Aunt Fran said, on the way out.

I closed the door after her and went to the kitchen to sit at the kitchen table and look out the window. The bird feeders were empty;

it was my father who kept them filled. I saw that his vials of pills were still lined up. I picked up his antihypertensive, thought about how his were probably the last hands to touch it. *Stan Meyer. Take as directed.* My eyes filling, I put the pills back in place and went out into the yard. I was leaning over to admire the infrastructure of the tulips when I heard the screen door slam. Steve flopped down on one of the patio chairs, and I moved to sit next to him.

"Hot out here," he said. And then, "What do you think, Laura? Is this really necessary?"

"Seems to be. For her."

"But what are we supposed to do?"

"Just listen, for starters. Just let her say all she needs to say. And then . . . well, I don't know. Tell her the truth, I guess. Tell her what you saw or didn't see."

"I didn't see anything. I told her that."

"Well, maybe if we hear more, we'll remember something. She's just looking for some sort of validation. That's what she said."

He looked at his watch, leaned back, and closed his eyes. Then he raised his chin and opened a few buttons on his shirt.

"Tanning?" I asked.

"Might as well."

"It's bad for you."

"Yeah. I like things that are bad for me."

We sat in silence for a while, and then I said, "Do you miss Dad?"

"Aw, man." He sighed, shook his head. "I don't even have his death on my screen yet. You know? I haven't really realized he's gone. When I think about him dying I feel bad, but I haven't really missed him yet. But I will. I know I will."

I heard the phone ring inside, and ran in to answer it. When I came out, I told Steve, "Caroline. She wants to come over now. Forget about dinner. Or get dinner later. Whatever. I told her all right." I didn't tell Steve she was coming from her therapist's office. That made me nervous; it felt as though both of them would be showing up.

He stood. "Good. Let's get it over with."

We went inside and sat in the living room, both of us with our arms crossed, I noticed. Both of us silent. Finally, I laughed out loud. "We're so grim!"

"Well, this *is* grim."

"I suppose. But you know, I heard this couple on the plane arguing about whether or not world peace will ever be possible. He said no; she said yes. Finally he said, 'Do you *really* want world peace?' She said, 'Of *course!*' He said, 'Can you learn to get along with your mother?' And she said nothing. Maybe the guy's right. Maybe we all need to clean up our own backyards. Maybe it's as important for us to talk about this as it is for Caroline."

"I don't think *anything* is as *anything* as it is to Caroline."

"Whoa. *What?*"

"You know what I mean. She's such a fucking drama queen!"

"Well, maybe we'll find out why." I smoothed away a nonexistent wrinkle in my pants.

Steve looked at his watch again. "You want to watch TV till she gets here?"

"Sure." Together we went to the family room, where we debated over whether we should order a set of frying pans, the likes of which would apparently never be offered for this incredibly low price again. And then we heard the door opening and I reached for the remote, clicked off the TV.

Caroline walked in and leaned against the doorjamb, pushed her sunglasses up high on her head, crossed her arms. "Hi. Thanks for coming." She was wearing black pants and a beautiful turquoise top. I wanted to compliment her on it, but now wasn't the time, I supposed. Still, I secretly studied the intricate pattern of the trim running along the bottom of her blouse.

"Want something to drink?" I asked her. "Or eat?"

"No, thanks. Could we sit in the living room?"

We walked past her single file, Caroline bringing up the rear. I felt as though Steve and I were children being sent to the principal's office. I was overly aware of the back of my neck, sure my defensiveness showed there. I thought about a friend of mine whose parents never once said they loved her and never praised her, thinking it would go to her head. *"Who do you think you are?"* they liked to say. One day when she was in her forties, she was over there for something, sitting at the kitchen table, and her father came up behind her, put his hand on her shoulder, and said, "We love you." And it made her feel like vomiting. She said it was just like that, she could feel something rising in her throat, and she thought she might throw up. She had sat immobile, wanting him to just go away. Out of the corner of her eye, she could see his fingers, yellowed by nicotine, the nails too long. She wouldn't look at him; she had remained absolutely still until he took his hand away and shuffled out of the kitchen. She said she had wanted to scream after him *It's too late!* but of course she did not. She'd just sat there until he was out of the room, and then she went home. He'd never mentioned it again, nor did she. She wept the day he died, but she said she cried only for the waste in his life, for the shame there was in that.

Imagine a different scenario: She puts her own hand on top of her father's. How hard would that have been? How hard *would* it have been? Here's who knows: only the woman herself. And maybe her father. Maybe him.

"ALL RIGHT, I JUST WANT TO SAY SOMETHING," Steve told Caroline. He had been patiently listening to a litany of complaints, delivered in an odd, nearly detached way by our sister. But now he said, "We didn't have a family like some others. Our father didn't bounce us on his knee. Our mother didn't sit us at the kitchen table after school and give us homemade cookies. Neither one of them had heart-to-hearts with us. We didn't call good night to each other at bedtime, like the Waltons. But what we had, *we had,* you know? There were things you could depend on. I mean, remember that summer we went to camp? I got a letter from Mom or Dad every day. Every single day!"

Caroline said nothing, stared into the space before her.

"Didn't you?" Steve asked, and I could see his wariness, his regret at revealing yet another thing he got from our parents that Caroline might not have.

Still, she said nothing.

"Did *you?*" he asked me, and I shrugged and nodded: yes.

Finally, Caroline said, "I didn't go to summer camp."

"Yes, you did!" I said. "We all did, just that one summer; we all went to different camps, remember?"

"You and Steve went," she said. "I didn't. I went to a hospital."

"For what?" I asked. Now, this I would have to have known. Why would I not have known this?

A long silence. And then Caroline said, "Because my mother came after me with a knife, and I was having a hard time dealing with it."

I sat wide-eyed and then felt a grin come on my face, an unfortunately misplaced expression of absolute astonishment, of horror. I covered my mouth.

"Okay, that's it," Steve said, and stood up. Then he sat back down. "Jesus, Caroline! I know you're lying! You went to summer camp! You came back with . . . I don't know, didn't you make a wallet or something?"

"Yes. At the hospital." She turned to Steve. "You and Laura weren't home. It was Sunday and we were going to have fried chicken for dinner. Mom was cutting up the chicken with a big butcher knife, and she got mad at something I said and raised it up over me. She said,

"I swear . . . I *swear*," and the knife was shaking in her hand. I was crouching on the floor, my arms over my head. The radio was on in the kitchen; I could hear some men talking and laughing. And then Dad came in the room and yelled her name and she spun around and said, "*What?* What do you expect me to *do* with her?"

I said, "But why, Caroline? Had you done anything to—" I stopped and wished I could grab back the words. Blame the victim. Great. I started again. "If this is true, why do you need us to verify anything? Why don't you just . . . I mean, there must be records."

"Remember the fire at St. Mary's?"

I did remember now: the summer of my junior year of high school. It was a spectacular fire; you could smell smoke miles away. "Yes," I said quietly.

"So. What I have is my memory of being there for a while. That's all. I don't remember the names of anyone who treated me. And no one but Dad knew I was there."

I saw my father in his hospital bed, almost telling me about someone being in the hospital and then deciding not to. Is this what he meant? *Oh, Dad,* I thought.

"It was after I came home that she finally stopped doing things to me. I think it scared her."

"But Caroline," I said, "how could they send you back home when you were in such danger? Why wasn't our whole family investigated by social services or something?"

"Because at a family meeting at the hospital, Mom denied everything. And the doctor believed her. And Dad said I had a tendency to exaggerate, a pretty wild imagination. That I seemed to gravitate toward the melancholy, the melodramatic—wink, wink." She leaned back in her chair, made a gesture of futility. "After that meeting, Mom went home and Dad took me to the hospital cafeteria to buy me an ice cream. Pretty cheap payoff, huh?"

"Oh, man." Steve rubbed his head. I thought I knew what he was thinking: *But you did gravitate toward those things.* It was, of course, what I was thinking as well.

Caroline smiled coolly. "I'm sorry this is so hard for you. And I'm not being sarcastic, I really mean it. But could you . . . I would like, finally, to feel that I can be supported by my brother. You are my brother."

"Well, what then, Caroline? What do you want me to do?"

She leaned forward. "Say you believe me. That's all."

He looked around the room, shaking his head. "You know, this is like—"

"Fine," she said. "If you can't, you can't. At least I tried."

"I didn't say I don't believe you!" Steve said. "I just said . . . I'm just trying to tell you it's a shock, that's all!"

"It is, Caroline," I said. "I can say that I do believe you; but it's really hard to take in. We thought you were in camp. They told us we were all going to camp!"

Steve's cell phone rang. He reached instinctively for it but let it go. We all sat still, listening to it ring a few more times before it stopped.

"Well," Steve said, "I just want to say I'm sorry for anything I might have done to make it worse. I know I never paid much attention to you—or to Laura, either, actually. I guess I was off in my own world."

"I guess we all were." I asked Caroline, "Are you staying here tonight?" Maybe after a few hours, we'd be looser, better able to talk.

"No. Bill and I are trying—"

"Oh, good. I'm glad, Caroline."

"Let me finish. We're trying to work out the details of a divorce agreement."

Steve and I looked quickly at each other, and I assumed we were sharing the same thought: *Oh, no, not more!* I remembered seeing a film once where one bad thing happened after the other; things just kept getting worse and worse. "That would never happen in real life," I said to Pete afterward. "*Something* good would be in there *somewhere.*"

Fatigue in Caroline's face was mixed with a kind of relief. I supposed the good here was that she had finally revealed the abuse she endured to the people she needed to tell. Except for one: the person responsible for it.

It is a family photo that a stranger must have taken, somewhere around the mid-sixties. We are all outside, at a park. There is a big wicker basket on a picnic table behind us. I remember that basket. It had a wooden top and a lovely dark-green pattern of trim—little x's—all along the edges. It must have been a cool day; the sky is overcast, and we are all wearing light jackets. Steve and I stand smiling before my father, leaning back into him. Steve has a baseball bat at his feet; I hold a stick that I must have meant to use for roasting marshmallows. My father, smiling broadly, proudly, has one hand on each of our shoulders. Caroline stands before our mother, and it is one of the rare times she is smiling. Our mother stands straight-mouthed behind her, arms crossed tightly across her chest, like a little kid in a store who's been told, Don't touch.

# 18

STEVE AND I WENT FOR DINNER TO A FAST-FOOD BURGER joint at the airport. It was Tessa who'd tried to call him earlier—she'd come down with something, and although she didn't feel sick enough to go the doctor, she was in need of some caretaking. Steve was only too willing to fly home and tend to her. He finished his hamburger, scrunched the wrapping into a tight ball, fired it at the nearby wastebasket, missed. He laughed and went to pick up his trash and deposit it from closer range. "About my yearbook aspiration to be a basketball star?" He sat back down, looked at his watch. "I should get to the gate pretty soon. God, what a trip this has been! You come home for a simple family visit, and all hell breaks loose. How are you doing with all this?"

"Oh, I'm fine. I've got Pete and the kids, and . . . you know, my life at home." I folded my napkin in half, then in fourths, offered a quick smile. "So." Not the real answer.

The real answer was, I didn't know how I was doing. I felt numbed by all I'd been told, and I went back and forth about what to believe, sometimes minute to minute.

"How can you suffer abuse like that and not tell someone—a teacher or a minister—a friend? Not that she had many friends. But you could tell *someone*. What about you and me? If we couldn't see what was happening, why didn't she just *tell* us?"

"You heard how much help she got from Dad and the doctor. And the three of us weren't exactly close. Anyway, she told me she actually believed it was her fault, that she caused that behavior in Mom."

He shook his head. "Even so. I just don't see how you can keep being around a person who treats you that way and not say something. It doesn't make any sense."

"I know." I stared at the table next to us, at the three little children sitting with their parents and eating their hamburgers. They were remarkably quiet and well behaved. One of them held a sock monkey, and she offered it a bite of her burger. Seeing this, something suddenly occurred to me.

"Steve? I wonder. Maybe what happens in these situations is the opposite of what we think."

"What do you mean?"

"Did you ever read about those monkeys they used in an experiment to measure love?"

"You can't measure love."

"Well, I know; I don't think so either. But this was . . . *did* you read about them?"

"Not that I recall."

"I saw it in the newspaper. What happened is that researchers in a primate lab put baby monkeys in with crazy mothers—cloth mother monkeys that had soft bodies so they could cuddle, but they were all booby-trapped. They would unexpectedly do something awful when the babies clung to them. One shook the baby violently, and one blew air out really hard on top of the baby's head, and one had brass spikes embedded in her chest that would all of a sudden pop out. You know what the babies did when those things happened? Clung tighter, if they possibly could. Or if they were thrust off by the force of what was done to them, they got up and ran right back."

Steve stared at me. "How can anyone work in a place like that?"

"Steve. The point is, the babies *clung tighter* when they were abused!"

"Caroline didn't cling tighter. She's really cold with Mom."

"*Now* she is. But remember when she used to idolize her? When she used to buy her all those presents and—"

"We're not monkeys, Laura."

"Sure we are."

He stood, pushed in his chair. "I've got to go. Want to walk with me to security?"

I walked beside him quietly, and then, just before we reached the line, I told him about a woman I once lived next door to who was sexually abused by her father in ways too horrible ever to repeat. And yet when I went over one day to borrow some coffee from her, there the man was—sitting on the sofa, reading a book to his two-year-old granddaughter. And the woman introduced me to her smiling father like she adored him. "So there you are," I said.

And Steve said, "Okay, I'll call you soon." He hadn't heard a word I'd said. Too full of things to listen anymore. Or too tired. Or something. And I didn't blame him.

I went out to the rental car I'd taken over from Steve, put the key in, and then sat there, thinking. I remembered something else about those monkeys. The abused babies were so preoccupied with reaching their mothers, they had no energy for friends, no time for trying to bond with anyone else. They were on a kind of psychological island, stuck with something that would never give them what they needed. The article ended by saying that every mother has the assurance that her baby will love her. But a baby has no assurance at all of being loved in return.

Tomorrow I would buy a cell phone. Times like this, I really did need one. I would call Pete, and when I heard his familiar voice, I would close my eyes and listen only to him.

BACK AT MY MOTHER'S HOUSE, I wandered around the quiet rooms, looking at the place in a way I hadn't for a long time. When I lived there, I saw it one way: home. It was a fact as irrefutable as the nose on my face. It was a personalized haven where I could get my needs met, though surely I didn't think of it that way. Rather, I thought of it as a repository for my things, a place where Velveeta cheese was kept on the refrigerator door and extra bottles of Pepsi in the laundry room. There was a big metal box of Band-Aids in the medicine chest, a never-ending supply of clean towels stacked in the linen closet. There was a desk in my room at which I did my homework, a living room where, in the evenings, my father sat in his chair under deep yellow lamp light with a library book, his shirtsleeves rolled up, his legs crossed in a way I came to find effeminate.

After I left home, I saw my parents' house another way: a place full of memories that dimmed year by year if not month by month, a place decorated in a way I would never consider, and then a place where I needed to be overly mindful of what my children were doing even after they were no longer young.

Now I stood in my parents' bedroom, thinking about what their life together was really like. I recalled various things we kids witnessed—the kisses hello and goodbye, the stereotypical sharing of household tasks—and I wondered about what we didn't see.

I moved over to their bed and sat down on it. What did they talk about before they went to sleep? Did they share corny rituals, as Pete and I do? Did they argue in hushed tones more often than we knew, turn angrily away from each other and pretend to be asleep until they actually were, then awaken in the morning with the psychic hangover that such resentment brings?

I took off my shoes and lay down on the bed, on my father's side. His nightstand still held the things he had kept there: the brown alarm clock, a "man-sized" box of Kleenex, an ashtray in which he kept not ashes but pennies. I closed my eyes, whispered *Daddy?* Nothing but a silence so profound I could feel it pressing against my ears.

I went to my mother's dresser and stared at myself in her mirror. This is what she looked into when she got up every morning. And what did she see now? Herself, alone, fifty years older than the time she bought this dresser. What a difficult transition she would have, going from a woman who was openly and exuberantly adored to one who lived in echoing silence. No one would be constantly complimenting, reassuring, and supporting her, as my father had. Or protecting her—perhaps egregiously. He was forever giving everything to her, and she was forever taking it with a kind of entitlement that used to make me furious. *Give something back!* I would think, but she did not, not really. She washed his underwear; she prepared meals; she stacked his mail on the dining room table. And she stayed beautiful.

I pulled open one of the top drawers. Bras and panties, folded neatly. In the drawer below that, negligees. This surprised me. I'd never seen her in one. I lifted the top one up, a light blue, with a matching peignoir. It looked brand new. Which accounted, I supposed, for my never having seen it. I was pulling out another drawer when the phone rang. I jumped, slid the drawer back in quickly, and went to the kitchen to answer it.

"What are you doing?" Maggie asked.

"You want the truth?" I sat down, smiling, grateful to hear her voice.

"Of course!"

"I was snooping in my mother's drawers."

"Find anything good?"

"Only a negligee. Matching peignoir."

"Excellent score."

"I think she just bought it. Isn't that weird?"

"Nothing's weird about what people do when someone close to them dies. And anyway, if she's like *my* mother, it's not new. It's just that she never wore it. 'Too good to wear.'"

"That wouldn't be my mother's problem. Speaking of which, what's happening at my house?"

"Well, your mother made her famous coconut cookies today. Anthony brought me some. He said they're famous because it's the only thing she makes that tastes good."

"That's pretty much right."

"And Hannah came home with a posse of girlfriends—I saw them all traipsing in as Anthony was heading out. So life over there is pretty normal, I'd say. How are *you* doing?"

I contemplated telling her everything but decided against it. "I'll tell you about it when I come home. Another couple of days here ought to do it."

"Well, I just wanted to check in."

"I'm glad you did."

"I wanted to know if you were all right. Are you—really?"

I hesitated, then said, "Yes."

"Just don't want to talk about it?"

"I guess not, Maggie. Not yet."

"Okay. Well, I'll see you soon. Call me anytime you want. Any time."

As soon as I hung up, the phone rang again. I picked it up, laughing, said, *"What?"*

"Hello?"

Steve. "Oh, hi!" I said. "I thought you were Maggie. Are you home?"

"Yeah, I am."

"How's Tessa?"

"She's got the flu, but it's the dry variety."

"What's that mean?"

"You know. No body fluids."

"Oh. *That's* good."

"Listen, Laura, I want to tell you something. I took a nap on the plane, and when I woke up, maybe even before I woke up, I was thinking about . . . well, I remembered something. And I wanted to tell you to tell Caroline."

"Me? Why, what is it?"

"Okay, this was . . . I don't know, I guess I was about five, because I remember Caroline was in first grade, and Mom got a call from the school nurse, and she had to go to school to get Caroline. And she was really mad. I went along, of course, and all the way she was muttering about how she guessed she knew her own child. But we picked up Caroline and she really *was* sick, so pale, and she just lay on the backseat of the car all the way home, didn't say a word. I remember thinking there was something kind of *off*, but I didn't know what. Now I think . . . you know what I think it was? I think maybe Caroline told Mom she was sick that morning, and Mom made her go to school anyway. And I think the nurse must have yelled at Mom."

"But Steve, why don't you tell Caroline all this?"

"Aren't you going to see her again tomorrow afternoon?"

"Yeah, but—"

"Just . . . tell her I remembered those things, okay? For what it's worth. Tell her I don't think she's crazy. I don't want to get into some huge—I just want her to know I don't *disbelieve* her. Would you tell her?"

"All right."

"And I'll . . . you know, I'll call her sometime soon. I will."

"Okay. Give my love to Tessa."

I hung up the phone and went outside, sat on the back steps, and looked up into the night sky. He wouldn't call her. He was out of it now. I knew him. He'd be at his bar tonight, slapping the backs of his male patrons, charming the females. Talking about the White Sox and Daley. Not for him the mess of all this. I have a personal theory about why most men walk away from difficult emotional situations: It's because they don't have babies. It is bred in them to leave the dwelling place to hunt and gather, to be outward-oriented; it is bred in women to lie down and give birth and stay home in order to care for the small world they have delivered into the larger one. Men conk things on the head or are conked themselves; women work out the kinks of the inner life.

I wished the fair weren't over. I wished I could sit outside and watch fireworks, blossoms of light in the darkness that would carry me up and away from myself. Instead, I thought of Caroline, of the life she had lived in this house: murderous rages and then a pork-chop dinner that night, with a mother whose face gave away nothing, with a father blinded by love, and with two siblings focused on anything but her. After such a dinner, days of relative peace, perhaps weeks. But I wondered if those peaceful times were any easier to bear, since she must always have been waiting for the next thing to happen.

I needed out of there. I looked at my watch—still early. I'd drive over to the huge bookstore a few blocks away, have an iced coffee, and look at some science books. There was a client who wanted a quilt made into linking chains, "kind of like DNA," she'd said. "You know what DNA looks like?" What it looks like is interesting. What it does is fathomless. But it is only a part of what makes us into who we become.

IN THE COFFEE SHOP OF THE BOOKSTORE, two women about my age sat at the table next to me. "I think it's hormones," one of them said. "I'm just feeling so emotional. On the way here, I saw a blind man trying to cross the street. I wanted to help, but I didn't want to offend him if he didn't need me. So I just watched him for a while. He was listening to the traffic so carefully, his head cocked, and—anyway, finally I just took his arm and said, 'It's okay to cross now,' and he smiled at me—this radiant smile—and it made me feel like bawling. I don't know why."

"It *is* hormones," her friend said. "I have days like that, when my skin feels peeled back, when I feel completely exposed. And on those days, I cry over everything: Hallmark commercials, dropping a dish . . . it's those damn hormones."

But I wondered if it wasn't something else. Maybe it was the tender irony of the way that we, blind ourselves, offer our arm to others, hoping to ease the crossing. Maybe it was the odd surges of love one can feel for an absolute stranger. Or maybe it was the way we give so little when it's in us always to give so much more. Thomas Merton wrote about feeling a sudden awareness of a profound connection to others, understanding that "they were mine and I theirs." I always loved reading things like that, things that pointed to our oneness and, by extension, our responsibility to others. It's the execution of anything specific that's the problem. It's kneeling down to meet the eyes of someone slouched on a sidewalk that you'd so much rather walk past. It's bothering to listen with an open heart to someone who smells bad. It's hard.

*The three of us kids are in a bathtub piled high with soap-*
*suds. In the background Steve and I are grinning happily. I*
*have made a lavish upsweep, using the thick lather of White*
*Rain shampoo. Steve has made devil horns. My knees are up*
*against my chest, my arms spread out wide—I remember*
*I was being Dinah Shore, singing "See the USA in your*
*Chevrolet." Steve has his hands behind his head, "wewax-*
*ing." In the foreground sits Caroline, solemn-faced, wide-*
*eyed, dry-headed. Her eyes are raised as though in silent*
*appeal to the person above her. She wants to be lifted up.*
*She does not want to be there.*

# 19

IN THE MORNING, I MADE A POT OF COFFEE. I'D HAVE A cup, and then do some handwork on the quilt I'd brought along, the one for the woman I met with just before I left. It was *for* a dog, as it turned out. That would eliminate any sew-ons, which the dog could eat. Instead, everything would be incorporated into the design of the quilt. I'd suggested some appliquéing, which would lessen the cost, but the woman thought appliqué was tacky.

I'm always amazed at how much people spend on their animals. I've never understood that kind of love, though I don't denigrate it. Maggie has a mutt that looks like a poodle in the front and an extraterrestrial in the back, and she worships him. Every Friday night he gets an Italian beef sandwich from Johnny B's.

When the coffee was ready, I went to the refrigerator for milk. I didn't see any—where did Aunt Fran put it? I saw a carton of cottage cheese, a package of English muffins that, though unopened, had passed its expiration date. Some Tupperware dishes holding leftovers. And that was it. I looked in the freezer, thinking she might have absentmindedly put it there. Nope.

I searched the cupboards for fake creamer, found none. It might be Dunkin' Donuts time. But first I'd call Aunt Fran.

When she answered the phone, I said, "Hey, you! Where's the milk?"

"Who is this?"

"It's me, Laura. I thought you brought us some milk. I don't see any."

"Well, yes, that's . . . listen, honey, is Caroline there with you?"

"No. I'm going to see her for lunch today. Why?"

"I wonder if I could ask you to come here first."

"Sure. Is something wrong?"

"Well, I just want to . . . I think there's something you should see."

"Okay. I'll be there in half an hour."

I dressed and got in the car, headed for the drive-through window of Dunkin' Donuts. If I didn't go in, I wouldn't be tempted to get a doughnut. When I spoke my order into the silver box, I requested a large regular coffee, skim milk, light, no sugar. "Anything else?" a voice asked, and I paused, then said, "A bowtie?"

On the way to Aunt Fran's, I passed a sign for a backyard play posted to a telephone pole. Aunt Fran once had a role in one of our backyard plays (to which Steve sold tickets, ten cents for a show and a paper cup of Kool-Aid), and she played a wicked witch so convincingly that one of the little kids in the audience went home crying and the mother called my mother to complain. I tried to remember the last time I stayed over at Aunt Fran's. I believe it was a summer night when I was fourteen. She helped my cousins and me write letters to stars that night. Gregory Peck was her choice, Paul McCartney was mine. Everyone I knew loved either Paul or John, except for Caroline, who preferred Ringo.

When I knocked at the door, it took a long time for Aunt Fran to answer, but then there she was, in her bathrobe. "I was just getting out of my gardening clothes," she said. "I'll be with you in a minute. Go in the kitchen, there's a big plate of chocolate chip cookies."

"Did you bake this morning?" I asked.

"No," she called, from her bedroom. "Brunderman's Bakery."

"I'm disappointed," I said.

"Eat one," she answered. "You won't be disappointed anymore."

Since I had already ruined my "diet," I ate two. Then, as I was pouring myself another glass of milk, Aunt Fran came into the room, carrying something under her arm. A small photo album, it looked like.

"*Here's* the milk," I said, holding up the carton and smiling at her.

"Sit down, Laura."

"Okay." I put the milk back in the refrigerator and sat down at her little kitchen table. There was a pitcher of flowers in the center, a beautiful arrangement from her garden: hydrangeas, lilies, small roses, all in shades of pink, a little baby's breath here and there, not the nearly yellow, defeated kind sold in grocery stores but bright little white blossoms, full as miniature petticoats.

She sat opposite me and put the photo album between us. "I didn't go over to bring you food the other day. I went over to get this out of the house. Your mother asked me to."

I recalled the brief bit of conversation I heard between the two of them. No wonder my mother hadn't wanted me listening in; she must have been talking to Aunt Fran about Caroline making trouble again. And she must have wanted her sister to remove anything that could get Caroline going.

"What is it?" I reached for the album, but Aunt Fran pulled it closer to herself.

"Your mother does not want you to know about this. But I've decided you should. I hope it's the right thing to do. She just never wanted you to know."

"About what?"

She opened the album to the first page, to a photo of a newborn in a crib. "Is that me?" I asked.

"It's your sister."

"Caroline."

"No. It's your sister who died. Her name was Claire."

I looked up quickly at Aunt Fran and then back at the baby. She was remarkably thin.

"She died when she was only nine weeks old."

"From what?"

"A heart defect. She never had a chance, really. It just about killed your mother."

I looked at the photo again. The baby was so young, it was hard to see much in her face. And her eyes were closed, her fist close to her face. I turned the page: more photos, the old-fashioned kind with jagged edges. There were only about twelve in all, some with my mother or father, one with another baby. "That's me, right?" I said, pointing to a picture with an older baby, staring in a direction opposite my sister.

"Yes, that's you. I wonder—I've always wondered, really—do you have any memory of that child?"

I shook my head. "No."

"You weren't even two when she died."

"I don't remember anything."

"Well, I wouldn't expect you to. And that's certainly the way your mother wanted it."

"Why?"

"The only way she could get past it, finally, was to deny it. But then when Caroline was born—too soon, really; it was much too soon for your mother to have another baby—she . . . well, it made all the sorrow come back. She saw Caroline healthy, and it reminded her of Claire, dead. And I think it affected the way she treated Caroline."

I nodded my head slowly, though I didn't really buy this explanation. It seemed to me that if you lost a baby you'd be overjoyed to have another one.

"At first it was just that she was afraid to get close, thinking it could happen again. Or maybe it was postpartum depression, which everybody talks about now. We didn't know about it then. But Laura, despite the way things were between them, you must know she does love Caroline."

"Pretty long time for a postpartum depression to last, Aunt Fran. And pretty selective behavior on my mother's part." I stared into the open face of a lily, all its parts exposed. Then I said, "Do you know that Caroline was in the hospital when she was a kid? She was there because—"

"I know," Aunt Fran said. "Your father and I both knew, though your father thought he was the only one. It was a terrible thing. But at least Caroline got some help. Things got better after that."

"But . . . what about my *mother*? What about help for *her*?"

"Things were very different then. People relied more on their own resources. I think your mother felt that if Caroline got help, she would be helped too."

"That makes no sense at all."

"It was a long time ago." Aunt Fran turned the photo album toward herself to look at the pictures. "She was a beautiful baby. And smile? That baby smiled from the day she was born. I swear, she was the happiest little thing you ever saw. And then came Caroline, such a sad little girl. Always so sad. I think your mother saw that sadness and it bothered her, that the one who lived would be so—"

"But Aunt Fran, my God! Caroline had reason to be sad!"

"Oh, I know. I know. But I often wonder which came first. Who caused what in whom. She closed the photo album. "Anyway. May I ask you to keep this a secret?"

"I . . . don't think I can. I'm sorry."

"Well, Laura, I showed you this so that when Caroline complains about her life, you know part of the reason that your mother had difficulty with her. And the other part, I must tell you, was Caroline herself. She was a difficult child. Surely you remember that! She remains difficult today; that woman cannot settle down inside herself. I love her, truly, but she is a tortured soul. It is not easy to be around her—not then, not now. You've had good luck with your children, Laura. I don't know if you've ever thought about what it would be like to have a child like Caroline.

"I really don't think your telling others about Claire will help anything. It might make things worse. Your mother made mistakes, but she tried her best to take care of all of you. That's all a parent can do."

I stood. "I've got to go."

She took hold of my arm. "I will ask you again to keep this a secret, Laura. It was your mother's wish that you kids never know. Not only so that she could try to forget about it, but so that you children wouldn't have to know about such a sad event. She wanted to protect you; she still tries to protect you. Don't remind her of things she tried so hard to forget and then, on top of that, tell her that her sister betrayed her—not when her husband has just died. Please, Laura."

"I won't say anything right now. That's all I can promise."

What I meant was, I wouldn't say anything to Caroline. But I was going back to my mother's house, and I was going to make a few calls. One to Pete for consolation; one to Maggie for advice. And then I would call Caroline, to tell her I was on the way to see her for lunch.

I drove home mindlessly, mechanically. The only thing I seemed to take in was a cemetery, which I noticed as I sat at a stoplight. Was Claire there? I wondered. I looked at one of the markers: a stone angel, bent at one knee, head hanging low, hands clasped over her heart, weeping tears of stone.

# 20

from Maggie. Pete thought I shouldn't say anything to Caroline; she was in such a fragile state that hearing what I'd learned might harm her further.

"But it might help her too," I said.

Pete said, "Well, it's hard to know how she would interpret it. So why take the risk?" I supposed he was right. I'd often been surprised by Caroline's reactions to things. And this was a delicate time.

Maggie told me she felt bad for me, handling all this alone. Which I realized I was, at least at this point. I told her to tell me something funny, to give me a yang for the yin. She said, "Hmm. Something funny. How about an Amazing Fact instead?"

"Fine."

"I used to be able to bounce a quarter off my stomach. Now I can hide an all-terrain vehicle in there."

"Sorry," I said. "I don't find that amazing. I find that funny. Also convenient. Next time we get tired on one of our walks, we'll just pull out your Hummer."

"Next time we take a walk, we'll be too old to walk."

"No, we really are going to start walking regularly."

"I know we are, sweetheart."

"As soon as I get back. I mean it."

"Hey. I'm lacing up my sneakers."

A FEW MILES FROM CAROLINE'S, I turned off the radio and listened to the sound of the rain that had begun. I turned on the windshield wipers and remembered, suddenly, a cabdriver I once had on a rainy night when I was visiting New York City. His wipers weren't working very well, the traffic was heavy, and he was in a terrible mood. I wanted to put a daisy down his rifle barrel, so I said, "Pretty bad traffic on Friday nights, huh?" "*Every* night!" he said, speaking from between clenched teeth. I looked across the backseat of the cab, as though seeking some sort of rolled-eye affirmation from an invisible ally. Then, in the warmest voice I could muster, I said "I guess it can be pretty hard to live here." We were at a stoplight, and I thought he might turn around and crack a smile. But he did not turn around. Rather, he began pounding his steering wheel. One fist, pounding steadily but slowly, terrible little intervals of silence in between. *Bam! . . . Bam! . . . Bam!* I got out then, said this was close enough, thank you very much, and gave the guy a really good tip, though he did not deserve one at all. I walked away thinking, What happened to this man? Why is he not like the cabbie I had earlier, who had a picture of his daughter on his dashboard, who pointed out tourist attractions in his thickly accented English, who sang a little song to himself as we waited for the light to change, who waved at and then laughed with another cabbie who pulled up beside him? Surely the angry man did not emerge from the womb shaking his fist. Who did this to him?

Pretty obvious memory to have pop into my head, as I drew closer to the house where my sister lived. Though of course what she pounded was not the steering wheel but herself.

CAROLINE WAS SITTING AT HER DRAFTING BOARD, looking at blueprints for an addition she was doing to someone's house. I looked at the finely drawn lines on the big white pages and said, "Funny how we both ended up doing kind of the same thing."

"What do you mean?" Caroline erased something, penciled in a correction.

"I mean, you know . . . making things out of raw materials. I use cloth, you use wood."

She looked up. "You know what I think? I think it's very different. I think I focus on seeing the actual substructure. You take things as they are and chop them up to re-create a new whole. And then you say, 'See? *That's* what it is!'"

"Meaning?"

"Meaning I want to know the truth of what's beneath. You want to transform things into something comfortable and beautiful, but not what they *are*." She stared at me, a little smile on her face. And then her smile faded and she said, "I'm sorry."

"It's all right."

"No, it's not. It's just . . . I'm in such a bad mood. I'm sorry."

"Maybe it's good for you to be in a bad mood."

She moved from her desk to sprawl out in a chair. "I'm so sick of this. I am. I am so sick of myself. You know what happened this morning? I toasted half a bagel. So far so good, huh?"

I smiled.

"And then I wanted to have it on a beautiful dish, I just wanted to have something beautiful to eat on because I'm trying to do what my therapist says and *nurture and reward myself.* So I have these cute little saucers I bought in an antiques store, cherries all over them, and I took one down from the cupboard, and here comes the big finger from the sky, pointing at me. *Put that back! That's a saucer! You can't eat a bagel on a saucer!* She looked up at me, sighed. "All the time, this voice: *Wrong. Stupid. That is not for you. It is for everyone else, not you.* And Laura, I want you to know, I really want you to be clear about this: It's not how I want to be. I look up at the night sky and see the same beauty you do. I mean . . . torch singers, little red potatoes, the sight of a kid running down the street with her tongue sticking out of her mouth . . . I *get* that.

"I want you to know that whenever I go to a museum, everything in my head gets pushed away. It doesn't matter what I look at : ancient pottery bowls, period rooms, sculptures—doesn't matter. The whole time I'm there, everything pecking away at my soul bows to greater considerations. I stand in front of a little French oil of a woman at a food market and all you can see is one slice of her cheek and her coat and hat and her shoes, and everything about her comes to me: where she lives, her little overheated apartment, the half circle of camembert wrapped in butcher paper in her refrigerator, the split in the lining of her shoe, the water level when she takes a bath, the little pink roses on her teacup, how she'll buy the lemons and the peaches—I see it all! I feel like I'm lost in the Wheel, only a part of some larger whole, and I can *breathe.* It's such a relief. But then I have to come out. I have to come back.

"What's wrong with me is what always intrudes. It overlies everything, that shadow. It's what never, ever, ever goes away. *No! You can't do that, you can't do that, shame on you, shame!* And I have had enough. I have had enough! I am going to give it a real try here,

I am by God going to try everything I can, and I am . . . I am . . . *No fear,* okay?" She pounded the arm of her chair at this last. Then she stopped, deeply embarrassed. "Jesus. Oscar clip. I'm sorry."

"Don't be sorry," I said, moving over to her, touching her am. "I'm glad you told me that. It makes me . . . well, it makes me know you." I looked at my watch. "Let's go out to lunch, want to? My treat. You can eat anything you want from anywhere you want it. I need to tell you something from Steve. And then I need you to tell me how I can help." *And then I want to go home.*

"I *WAS,* SICK," CAROLINE SAID. "And Steve's right. When I was lying on the cot in the nurse's office, I heard her kind of yelling at Mom. *Didn't you notice she had a fever, Mrs. Meyer?* I remember wanting to come home because I felt so bad and yet dreading it because I knew I'd be in trouble again."

I played with the few strands of pasta left on my plate. In it, I suddenly saw a kind of filigree design that was actually very beautiful. I started to say, "I'm listening to you, Caroline. But I just saw something here that I want to get down." I could feel heat rising at the back of my neck at the thought, at how close I came to pulling out my sketch pad, knowing that she would have said, in one way or another, "It's okay. I don't mind."

Instead I said, "I . . . it must have been so hard for you." I cleared my throat. D+, I gave myself for that attempt at an empathic response. Beneath the table, my free hand curled into a fist.

Caroline smiled sympathetically. She could see I was ready to jump out of my skin. "Look. I know you've been trying very hard to . . . in the midst of . . ." She put her hand over mine. It was such an awkward gesture; I could feel the clamminess. Were we friends, were we real sisters, I could comment on this, say something funny, and it would be fine. As it was, I ignored what surely both of us were aware of, making the moment even more awkward than it already was. "I'm trying to say thank you. It means so much that you listened to me. And that you said you believe me." She took her hand away, put it in her lap. "So."

I moved closer to her. "So. What now? Do you still feel like you need to talk to Mom?"

"I know it's not the right time, with Dad . . .'"

"Probably not."

"And I've got lots of work to do in the meantime, God knows."

"I guess we all do."

"Thank you for coming back here, Laura. You can . . . why don't you go back home? I know it's hard for you to be away. But could I call you sometime?"

That she needed to ask. "Any time," I said, and a small black part of my heart singsonged, *You don't mean it.* "Any time," I said again, overcoming it.

I DECIDED TO PAY THE EXTRA COST and fly home that evening. Before I left for the airport, I called Aunt Fran. "I've been thinking," I said. "I would really like permission from you to tell Caroline and Steve what you told me."

"Oh, Laura."

"I think it might help. I think it might help everyone."

"She trusted me to never let you kids know."

"But look at what's happening. Caroline is having a lot of trouble right now, dealing with the way she grew up. I mean, she had a mother who attacked her with a knife, and she—"

*"What?"*

"Well, Aunt Fran . . . you know that. You said you knew. You said you knew! Mom attacked—or very nearly attacked—Caroline with a knife! That's why Caroline was hospitalized."

"Oh, honey. Oh my goodness. That's not true. It was the other way around! She came after your mother!"

"That's what my mother told you?"

"It was the other way *around*! Oh my goodness. Caroline said your mother attacked *her*? No, sweetheart, I swear to you, it was the other way around! Ask—oh, I was going to say ask your father. But he knew. It was Caroline who tried to attack your mother!"

There sat the spider, beautiful in her web, drops of dew shining like diamonds all around her. I spoke very carefully. "Aunt Fran. Do you honestly believe that?" I picked up a pencil from the kitchen table, balanced it along the knuckles of one hand while I waited for her answer. *Come on, Aunt Fran, you were my favorite. You in a yellow sundress, holding two of your own kids, one under each arm, laughing.*

"Well, of course I do! It's the truth!"

I let the pencil fall; it rolled under the table. I would not bother to retrieve it. My mother had Aunt Fran, just like she had my dad. There was no more to say. I held on to the phone and stared out the window at the sunset. Beautiful pinks. Dusty rose. Mauve. Wonderful next to sage green.

"Laura?"

"I have to go." I hung up the phone, locked my mother's house, and headed to the car to go to the airport. Enough. I turned on the radio, turned it up loud. Then louder still.

It is a travel advertisment in a newspaper, a half-page picture of an older couple in their late seventies or early eighties, floating in a pool on rubber rafts with built-in pillows. The water is crystal clear and shot through with jagged lines of sunlight. The man wears black bathing trunks that come almost to his knees, funny, in their way. The woman wears a beautifully designed swimsuit in a Hawaiian print with a plunging neckline that—unbelievably—looks sexy. Her necklace is made of shells that coordinate with the bathing suit. She wears a bathing cap covered with flowers but has left uncovered one perfect wave of streaked hair. Her husband holds her hand—it is he who has reached out to her; it feels somehow that it is always he who reaches for her. Her face is a study in pride: eyebrows plucked in a graceful arch, cheekbones high and rouged, lipstick perfectly applied. She has a smile on her face; his expression is more serious, nearly anxious.

When I came across this picture, I had an odd reaction to it. "Look at this," I told Pete, and he looked over and said, "Huh. Cute."

"It's not cute!" I said angrily.

Pete looked up, surprised.

"It's not! Look at her! This is a woman whose been overly cared for all her life. She's a user; she thinks only of herself. Look at her eyes!"

He looked again. "You can't even see her eyes."

He was right. Both people in the photograph wore dark sunglasses.

"Well, I know what they look like," I said.

"How?" Pete asked, and I did not answer, because I could not say.

# 21

PETE PICKED ME UP AT THE AIRPORT. HE LEANED OVER to give me a quick kiss before we pulled away from the curb. I wondered what he'd ask me and what I'd say. I realized I'd fallen once again into uncertainty. I was beginning to think I understood battered wife syndrome: seeing someone as a monster, then as someone not so bad, then as someone familiar and loved. "Damn it!" I said.

"What happened?" He slowed the car, checked the rearview.

"Nothing," I said, waving my hand. "Sorry. It's okay, don't stop. I'll tell you later. I don't even know what I'm feeling." I began to cry, which only made me angrier.

"Are you okay?"

"Yes. No. Oh, I don't know." I wiped away the few tears I'd shed. "Listen, can we go get a drink somewhere? Are the kids okay?"

"The kids are fine. Your mother's there. And . . . well, surprise, my parents are too."

I stared at him, open-mouthed. "When . . . ?"

"They didn't tell me. They were on their way back from some-where, and they were only fifty miles away. . . . They arrived just after your flight took off from Minnesota."

I leaned back against the seat and closed my eyes. "Pete. You know I love them. But so much is going on!"

"Let's go somewhere and talk."

"Somewhere close. I don't know why I'm angry. I'm not angry. I really am not angry."


THE CROWDED BAR WAS IN AN AIRPORT HOTEL, and many of the pa-trons had their carry-ons beside them. I had to squeeze past a large black overnighter to get into my seat. "Oh, sorry," a young woman said, pulling it in closer to her.

"No problem." I said this, though what I wanted to say was *Move it!*

Pete ordered wine at the bar and brought it back to the table. I said nothing until he reached over and rubbed my shoulder.

"What a mess!" I shook my head.

"Did something else happen?"

"You won't believe this. Aunt Fran told me—" I stopped talking, aware that the young woman I squeezed past was listening intently. "I'll tell you in a minute," I said. And then, pointedly, "Maybe we should switch tables."

With that, the young woman rose, put money down on the table, and stalked off.

Pete watched her go. "What was that all about?"

"She was eavesdropping."

"Ah."

"I hate it when people do that."

He said nothing, but in his silence I could hear his all-too-correct accusation: *You do it constantly.*

"Anyway, Aunt Fran told me it was Caroline who attacked my mother, not the other way around."

Pete sat back. "Wow. So what do you think?"

"At first, I was absolutely convinced that Fran was taken in by my mother in the same way Dad always was. But now I don't know. I can't think straight. I feel like I need to be doing something, and I have no idea what to do. I mean, I feel weird going home to see my mother, when I don't know if she . . . I don't know what to believe, Pete. I honestly don't."

"Maybe you just have to let things sit for a while. It's not like you have to make any decisions about anything right away. Whoever did what, it happened a long time ago. Caroline's said what she needed to say, and she's getting help. Your mother's okay for the time being. I think . . . well, I might as well tell you now, I think she wants to stay with us for a while. Lots of hints about how she feels glad to have company, how she can help with this and help with that."

"Help with what?"

"Oh, babysitting—"

"We don't need a babysitter. We finally don't need one!"

"Shopping, she mentioned grocery shopping."

"I like to pick out my own things."

"Laura?"

"What!"

"It's not *my* idea. She's not *my* mother. You know?"

"I know that!" I stared at him. "Oh, I'm sorry. I'm just mad. I want to go home and just have it be normal again. I don't want her there. That's the truth. And I miss my dad, and I haven't even been able to take the time to mourn him." I sighed. "I don't know, I guess you're right. There's nothing to do now but let some time go by. Let's just go home."

In the car, with the radio off, the quiet and the darkness and the presence of Pete began to soothe me. "I'm not going back *there* for a while!"

"You don't have to." He took my hand. "So. You want to know my thing that happened today?"

"What?" I turned toward him, nearly giddy with relief.


ROSA, SUBBY, MY MOTHER, PETE, and I were seated at the kitchen table, and the kids were upstairs in their rooms. We were having coffee and the excellent pistachio biscotti that Rosa baked this afternoon, probably fifteen seconds after she set foot in the house. We were all in our pajamas, and despite the strain of everything that had been happening, I felt happy. It was as though I'd awakened from a bad dream, had left behind a pulling darkness to join these familiar faces in this most familiar of settings. Our voices overlapped as we talked; we laughed frequently. What was notable, of course, was my father's absence, that persistent raw spot: my mother's smile fading as she rubbed the familiar bump of bone on the outside of her wrist the way she used to rub the knuckles of his hand.

Rosa's short gray hair was in pin curls, and she wore a black hairnet over them. She was talking about her father, how he used to stuff a sock and call it a cat. "He would hold it in his arms and pet it, *Goooood kitty, goooood kitty,* and then—MEOW!—he'd make it jump out of his arms. Oh, I'm telling you, we loved it. We used to laugh till we peed our pants."

"Today, these kids need cyberspace to be entertained," my mother said.

"They use it for their schoolwork too, though," Rosa said. "It's all right. They all find new things; every generation has its own new things."

From upstairs, I heard Hannah calling me, so I excused myself and went up to her room. She had the phone pressed to her chest. "Can I babysit for the Pearsons Saturday night? Their regular sitter canceled."

Hannah had never done this, though she did take a Red Cross course in babysitting. And the Pearsons lived just down the block and their children weren't all that young—maybe five and seven. "Sure," I told her.

Hannah held up a finger, asking me to wait, and said into the phone, "That will be fine. . . . Okay, seven o'clock. Thank you."

She hung up and beamed at me. "My first job. I'll get six dollars an hour!"

"That's great!"

"So . . . what do I do?"

"Do for what?"

"To babysit!"

"Oh! Well, you know, first and foremost, just make sure they're safe. That's why people hire babysitters, to make sure their children are safe. You remember what it was like, having babysitters."

"Yeah, I don't want to be like them, though."

"What do you mean?"

"They were boring. I'm going to be a fun one, like Mary Poppins."

"Okay," I said. "That's a noble goal."

"Did you babysit a lot, Mom?"

"I did." I went over to her bed, motioning for her to move so I could sit beside her. "I have to tell you, though, I was not one of the fun ones."

"Why not?"

"I don't know. I guess I thought I had to be a tough boss."

"Well, I'll be the boss, but I'll be a fun boss. Do you think I could take some things over to show them?"

"What things?"

"I don't know. Books. Maybe a game or two?"

Of course they would have their own. But I loved her enthusiasm. "I think that would be great."

"Okay. So . . . would you close my door?"

Dismissed.

I went out into the hall and then stood for a while at the head of the stairs. I could hear my mother talking about my father, describing the way he used to make shadow puppets on the walls for us. How much we used to love that. How none of us would ever agree on what he was making, and he would never tell, so that all of us could be right.

THE NEXT MORNING, I WAS STANDING at the cutting table in my studio when Rosa appeared. "We're going to take off in a little while."

I put down my rotary cutter and started upstairs.

"Oh, no, keep working; I just wanted to sit with you for a while."

"Good." I slid a chair over to her and returned to the mat, to slicing off three-quarter-inch strips from a bright yellow cotton print.

"Well, it's official: Subby is on the last hole of his belt. He's going to have to get suspenders."

I laughed. "That's what you get for being such a good cook. Anyway, I like suspenders."

"Oh, but he doesn't!"

"Why not?"

"Because his Uncle Yaya wore suspenders and he was such a mess! His pants wouldn't button anymore and his zipper was always a little bit open. Little bits of saliva always at the corners of his mouth.

He had a banged-up hat he would never take off, and his shirts always had stains on them. He was the kind of man, seemed like flies were always buzzing around him. They weren't, but it *seemed* like they were. And you know Subby, he likes to be so neat. Every day, with his hair cream and his cologne."

"Well, he doesn't have to look like his uncle just because he wears suspenders!"

"You know how it is. You have associations with things. But today I'm going to get him a nice pair of yellow suspenders; he'll love them. I saw them in Brooks Brothers. He doesn't know. I told him we had to go to the mall on the way out of town. He'll wait in the RV for me; he takes naps while I shop."

"You still like driving around in that thing?"

"Oh, it's wonderful. You make a lot of friends."

I smiled, sliced through more fabric, stacked the strips I'd cut into a pile.

"Laura? I want to ask you something. How are you doing with . . . how are you feeling?"

"I'm okay, Rosa. Thanks." I looked over at her, smiled.

"I remember when my father died, it was . . . I felt suddenly so alone in the world."

"Yes."

"It will take time, sweetheart."

"I know."

"So! I made you some sauce—it's in the freezer. Red gold."

"Thanks. I love your red sauce. I still can't make it like you."

"You have your own way. You're a wonderful cook."

"Rosa? I want to ask you something. If you heard something from a reliable source about someone else—" I looked at her, her wide gray eyes. "Okay. Suppose your sister told you something about your mother that you had a hard time believing. Would you—"

She held up her hand. "I think I know what you're going to say."

"You do?"

"Your mother and I have talked over the years about your sister. Not a lot, but enough so I know it isn't good between them. And of course I've been with Caroline a few times, and she's . . . well, she's—"

"I know. She's kind of hard. But Rosa, can I tell you something in confidence?"

I looked upstairs, guiltily, and Rosa said, "Your mother is sitting outside with Subby."

"Well, here's the thing. My sister told me about some things that happened between her and my mother, really terrible things."

"Show me a parent who says she hasn't made mistakes, and I'll show you a liar."

"But these were big mistakes, Rosa. Damaging mistakes. I don't know . . . well, the truth is, I don't know who to believe or how to handle this."

She sighed. "Okay. Show me a parent who hasn't made *damaging* mistakes."

"My sister says my mother came after her with a knife."

Rosa sat very still, then breathed out. "*Madonna.* Somebody is in big trouble."

It is someone's birthday party, I can't tell whose. There is a big cake in the middle of the kitchen table. My mother has cut a huge piece, the first piece, and is offering it to Caroline. There are butter-cream flowers on the slice she holds; a candle too—it is a prime piece of birthday cake. My mother's back is to the camera, her hand on her hip. Without seeing her face, you can guess at her expression. That is because you can clearly see Caroline's face, taut and unsmiling. Refusing what is offered her. It must be my father taking the picture; he is the only one not at the table. What he was attempting to document, I don't know. For Steve's and my part, we are tossing a balloon back and forth, over Caroline's head. For a long time, we have known that sometimes it serves you best simply to work around an obstacle, to make invisible what you are tired of seeing or don't understand.

# 22

IT WAS A CROWDED SATURDAY MORNING AT FABRIC WORLD, and Gregory was spending too much time searching out a fabric for me. He'd vaguely remembered seeing a dog-bone print in novelty fabrics, but now it was nowhere in sight. He looked through all the juvenile fabrics, then searched the back room. "Maybe somebody put it in with the black-and-whites," he said. "Let's go see."

I slogged along behind him, carrying an armload of bolts of fabric that had nothing whatsoever to do with what I was working on. "Put those *down*," he told me—again—and again I told him no. "What do you think, someone's going to come along and buy a whole bolt?"

"It could happen."

He bent down over a row of black-and-white prints and started going through them. "You know, my partner does that in bookstores. He always buys a lot of books at once, and he carries them around the whole time, this big stack of books. I tell him to put them *down,* and he says no, somebody might buy them. Like there's not more. Like he's holding on to the last copies. And even if he were, like he couldn't order others."

"I understand completely," I said. "That is the way things should be done."

He looked disapprovingly over his shoulder at me. "Hmmm. I suppose you're a firstborn."

"I am!"

"So is Raymond. You all are so bossy." He pulled out a bolt of fabric, a white printed with tiny black dog bones. "Voilà!"

I snatched it from him. "Oh, perfect! Thank you!"

"Come over to the table, I'll cut it for you myself."

"To what do I owe this great honor?"

He shrugged. "Friendship."

It was true. We were friends. And yet I'd never exactly thought of it that way. I sought out Gregory every time I came to Fabric World; I was disappointed when he wasn't there; we sat in his office and talked fabric and gossiped, yet until now I'd never really thought of him as a friend. It felt vaguely greedy to think of him that way, as though one were appropriated a certain number of friends and should not cultivate relationships beyond that. But that was ridiculous! And so, "Hey, Gregory," I said. "Would you and Raymond ever like to come to my house for dinner?"

"Ever? Is this a tentative invitation?" He whispered this last.

"No. It's a definite invitation."

"What night?" He began unwinding one of the bolts of fabric. "How much?"

"Three yards of each. And . . . I don't know. Any night."

"How's tonight? Because I know we couldn't do it otherwise for a couple of weeks. We're very popular, as you can imagine."

"I can."

He looked over the top of his glasses at me. "You're so easy. Actually, it's that we're going on vacation tomorrow. Two weeks in San Francisco, and I can't wait."

"Tonight? . . . Well, sure, why not? I have to warn you, though, my mother is staying with us."

He folded up the fabric he'd cut for me, leaned forward to say, "She'll love me."

"I'm not worried about that part."

"I'm sure I'll love her too."

I said nothing. Finally, he laughed and said, "Oh, so what?"

"Seven o'clock?" I said and he nodded, then rolled his eyes as he heard himself paged. "I hate it when you're at work and they make you work!" he said. "It's so unfair!"

AT FOUR O'CLOCK, I CALLED MAGGIE and asked her if she and Doug wanted to come to dinner as well. "Can't," she said. "We're already going out—with Doug's boss. I have to wear nylons and everything."

"Sorry."

"Has to be done."

"So tell me," I said. "If I use my mother-in-law's red sauce, do I have to confess it's not mine?"

"Who'll ask?"

"Gregory will. I can feel it in my bones."

"What's so wrong with saying it's not yours?"

"I don't know. I feel like if you invite people to dinner, you should make it yourself."

"That was in the olden days."

"Okay. Thanks for the reality check." I hung up and the phone rang immediately. It was Caroline.

"Hey," I said. "How are you doing?" I looked at the clock on the kitchen wall; I had to get busy on the lasagna. I should have let the machine pick up.

"I'm okay," she said. And waited.

I waited too, then finally asked, "So . . . things are going well?" I could hear the tension in my voice; I hoped she could not.

"Have you . . . do you know when she's coming home?"

"Mom?"

"Yeah."

"I don't. Soon, I would expect. I think she just felt like she needed to have people around her for a while. Why?"

"Oh, just—"

"Are you thinking you need to . . . do something with her?"

"I'm thinking I need to spend some time with her, yes."

"I don't know, Caroline. She hasn't said much about when she's going back. Listen, I'm sorry, but this is a really bad time. I'm having company for dinner, and—"

"Oh! Why didn't you say so? Never mind."

"Don't do that."

"What?"

"Look, I'm sorry, I just don't have time right now."

"Yes, I know. You told me. I heard." She hung up.

I stood for a while with the receiver in my hand, then put it back in the cradle. *Not this time,* I was thinking.

I took out the things I needed from the refrigerator and began chopping onion and garlic. Maggie was wrong; I had to make my own sauce. The door burst open and Anthony came in, followed by Hannah and my mother. In a way, my mother had moved from being my mother to another one of the kids. I kind of liked her like this. "Where have you guys been?" I asked.

"We took Grandma to Sam Goody's," Hannah said. "She got us CDs."

My mother leaned on the kitchen counter, watching me chop the onions. "What's for dinner?"

"Lasagna," I said. "We're having guests."

"Who?" Hannah asked, and when I told her, she wailed, "Nooo! I can't be here! I have to babysit!"

I'd forgotten, but I didn't want to admit this, so I said, "Well, there'll be another time."

"How do you know? You've never had Gregory here!"

"There will be," I said. And then, as the phone rang yet again, "Answer that, will you?"

Hannah picked up the phone, listened, and then said, "Oh, hi, I'm so happy you're coming!" Then, listening more, she said, "Oh, no! Really? Well, tell him he'll get better if he comes here!"

I wiped my hands on a dish towel and reached out for the phone. "Here's my mom," Hannah said. She grabbed her CDs and ran toward the stairs and her room.

"Who's Gregory?" I heard my mother ask Anthony at the same time that Gregory told me, "I'm going to kill Raymond. Don't tell anyone I did it. I'll try to be humane."

"What's up?" I said.

"He is *such* a hypochondriac! He's convinced he's having some *respiratory* problem. I have to take him to the ER, his home away from home."

"But *is* something wrong?" I asked, alarmed, and Gregory said, "No, no. It's nothing. It's never anything. He always does this before we go on trips. He gets anxious when we leave home. It is never anything, and it won't be this time either. He's always got something. And it's always something with a very grim prognosis." I hear him cover the phone with his hand and then he shouts, "I'm coming! Just start the car." He lowered his voice. "Last time the doctor said, 'Mr. Haley, why don't you just go home and get on with your life?' Listen,

I'm so sorry to cancel at the last minute. . . . Although I also invited myself at the last minute."

"It's okay," I said. "We'll do it another time."

"Can we?"

"Of course. Call me when you get back from vacation. We'll set something up."

"His real problem," Gregory said, "is that he just quit his job and now he's *between*. He doesn't know what to do with himself. He runs around vacuuming all the time. I mean, I'm gone all day and then I come home and I'm returning phone calls and he has to go and *vacuum*. I say to him, 'Uh, Raymond? Can you see that I'm—*Hold on, I'm coming!*'"

"You'd better go."

"Yes, on to macaroni surprise at the hospital cafeteria. I can't wait."

I hung up the phone, crossed my arms, stared at the lasagna pan. "Well, that's that."

"What? He can't come?" Anthony asked. "But can't you make it anyway?" Lasagna was Anthony's favorite food. He could easily put away half a pan for a single serving.

"I'll make it," my mother said. "Why don't you and Pete go out to dinner? You two could use a night out."

The idea of going out with Pete was very appealing—a dress-up date with my husband. Time alone.

"Go ahead, I'll feed the kids," my mother said. "Pick Pete up at work and surprise him."

I looked at my watch, then at her.

"Go!" she said.

Anthony stood and raised his arms up high, stretching. "Okay with me," he said. Fewer people equaled more lasagna.

I went upstairs and into Hannah's room. She was listening to her new CD with her headphones on, her eyes closed. I lifted up the headphones and told her, "I'm going to go out to dinner with Dad, okay? I know I said I'd be here when you babysat, in case you needed anything."

"I'm fine," she said. "I've got everything planned—they're going to love me, they're going to want me all the time. And anyway, Grandma will be here."

I changed clothes and all but skipped down the steps. I wouldn't tell Pete anything except that he had to come with me. Then I'd take him for a steak the size of Russia. We would talk about everything but the stone in my shoe.

ON THE WAY HOME FROM THE RESTAURANT, Pete turned off the radio and looked over at me. "Hey. Want to go make out?"

"I knew you'd like this outfit." I'd worn a red dress with a low neckline that I still looked pretty good in, and heels high enough to cause pain. All through dinner, I'd left them off my feet.

"I mean it. I know a place right near here."

"How do *you* know a place?"

"Watch." He made a few turns, and we pulled into the back lot of a grocery store.

"Very romantic," I said, gazing over at rows of wooden crates stacked up against a concrete wall, at a massive-sized Dumpster, the lid yawning open, heads of what looked like cabbage strewn across the top of a small mountain of garbage.

"This is what constitutes romance at our stage of the game: It's dark, and there are no other people." He tuned the radio to what passed as a jazz station and raised an eyebrow. "There will be absolutely no interruptions."

"You must have had more wine than I thought."

He pulled me to him. "I love my wife."

"Well. That's very nice."

Very slowly, he ran his hand up my leg. I started to laugh, to say, We're too old, this is ridiculous! But we weren't, and it wasn't.

When I was in grade school, I, along with the other girls, wrote boys' names on my notebook paper, wrote myself as *Mrs.* a hundred times in a dreamy script. But I did that in the same way that I wore whatever clothes were in style—I had no real belief that I would ever meet in the middle with someone. And indeed it did take a long time for me to find someone I wanted to marry. But I'm so glad I waited. What I know about Pete and me is that the flame will never go out. I do not look up from tossing the salad and think, *Oh, God, how the hell did I ever get here?* I do not look at the back of his head and think, *I don't know you at all.* I wake up with my pal, and go to sleep with my lover. He still thrills me, not only sexually but because of the way he regards the life that unfolds around him. I am interested in what he says about me and the children and our respective jobs, but I am also interested in what he says about the Middle East and the migratory patterns of monarchs and the amount of nutmeg that should be grated into the mashed potatoes and the impact that being a thwarted artist had on the life of Hitler. I believe Pete is a truly honest and awake and kind individual. If we live more than once, I want to find him again. The family I have made with him are my bunker and my sword. They are another form of oxygen: Without them, everything in me would shut down. It is terrifying to know that love can have such power. It is also gratifying.

AS WE TURNED DOWN OUR STREET, I saw the spastic flash of ambulance lights. I sat up straight and leaned forward, alarmed. "What's that?"

"It's not our house," Pete said. And then, "It's the Pearsons! Isn't Hannah babysitting for them?" Reflexively, a little drama played out in my head: me, telling Maggie, *Pete said, Isn't Hannah* . . .

We pulled up outside of the Pearsons and ran out of the car. There on the lawn were Hannah, the Pearson boy, and my mother. My mother was kneeling beside Tyler, talking to him. The ambulance attendants were putting a gurney with a small figure—Nicki— strapped in place into the back. There was a big bandage on her forehead. I ran over to them and asked breathlessly, "What happened?" The attendant who climbed in with Nicki leaned forward to close the door. "Not as bad as it looks, but we've got to go." The door slammed shut and the ambulance took off, siren wailing.

Hannah wept loudly, and Pete stood beside her, speaking quietly to her. I went over and put my arms around her. "Hannah, what happened?"

"I was giving Nicki a piggyback ride to bed," she gulped. "She leaned back, trying to reach for her stuffed animal, and I dropped her and she fell and cut her eye on the coffee table."

"She cut her eye?"

"Right beside her right eye," my mother said.

"Oh, Hannah." I pulled her closer, rubbed her back. She was crying so hard she was hiccuping. I looked over at Pete, who nodded at me, meaning he'd stay. I took her hand. "Come on, let's go home."

"I'll stay here," I heard my mother tell Pete. "You go with them."

Hannah cried until she exhausted herself. Nothing Pete or I said seemed to console her. Finally, leaving her in her room, Pete and I went downstairs. Just as we were collapsing into the sofa, the door slammed and my mother came into the room. "Mrs. Pearson is at the hospital; Mr. Pearson just came home. They said the girl will be all right. She can come home tomorrow." She sank into a chair.

"Do you think we should go over and talk to Jim?" I asked Pete.

"Wait till tomorrow," he said. "I think that will be better. I'll go with you first thing in the morning."

"What was he like?" I asked my mother. "Was he really upset?"

"Well, of course he was! Wouldn't you be?"

"Well, *yes*, but . . . what did he say?"

"Not much, really. Just listened to what happened and made sure his son was all right. I told him it was all Hannah's fault and apologized for her."

For a moment, I sat very still. Then I said, "What?"

She cocked her head brightly. A woman at a bridge table, her hand in the peanut bowl. Charms on her bracelet tinkling.

"What did you say?" I asked, my voice rising.

Confused, she looked over at Pete, who said, "Laura—"

"No!" I told him. And then, to my mother, "You told him it was all Hannah's fault?"

"It was!" She was angry now; twin patches of color appeared in her cheeks.

"It was an accident, Mom! She didn't mean to do it!"

"Well, I know that. But it was her *fault*!"

"Did you tell her that?"

She opened her mouth, closed it.

"Did you, Mom?"

"I may have said something like that. I mean, it was very confusing at first. I got a call; I went over there; the child was bleeding badly."

I stood, started to say something, but went instead upstairs to Hannah's room. I turned on her bedside light and saw her lying there, her eyes wide. "Honey? Listen. I know you feel so, so bad."

"Grandma's right; it's all my fault."

So she'd heard everything. "It was an accident, Hannah. You never anticipated such a thing would happen."

"I made her get a scar!"

"How do you know? They do things now that—"

"Grandma said. She said she'll have a big scar on her face her whole life!"

"Hannah, Grandma—she didn't really know what she was saying. She just said the first thing that came into her head. She was frightened, and she—"

"No, Mom! She's right! Don't you think I know that?"

Again, she began to sob, and I lay beside her and wrapped my arms around her. I was remembering the time she was four years old and I took her to a Kmart, telling her she could have any toy she wanted. She'd decided she wanted a doll, and we looked for a long time at all the options available: the long-haired high-breasted Barbies; the fancy baby dolls that talked and ate and wet; the ones that came with high chairs and playpens and dishes and toys; the delicate porcelain dolls with dresses made of lace and velvet, with prim, painted lips. And then Hannah found a doll lying along the bottom of a bin. She was not in a box, and she had a rip in her cloth body. "This is not a good one," I'd told Hannah. "This one is damaged." The doll was cheaply made; her eyes did not open and close, the fabric used to cover her body was thin and shiny, her plastic toes were more grotesque than endearing, and she came with not so much as a diaper. But Hannah pulled the doll to her breast. "I will call her Baby Annie," she'd said.

I remembered, too, a time when she was about the same age and Anthony had a play date, so Hannah and I decided to have a play date of our own. We were walking to the bus stop, on our way downtown, when we passed a tiny turquoise-colored egg on the sidewalk, not far from a tree. "What's that?" Hannah asked, squatting down to inspect it, and I told her it was a robin's egg. I did not say that it appeared that a cat had gotten at the nest or that perhaps the wind had knocked it down. I did not point out the fine crack running along its side. "Where's its mother?" Hannah asked, and I said, Oh, the mother would be back soon. We went downtown and bought new clothes at Hannah's favorite store. We had lunch and ice-cream floats at the dime-store lunch counter. We went to the library and spent over an hour selecting just the right books to bring home.

That evening, I'd sat her on a high stool to help me wash potatoes for dinner. The sun was setting; I remember admiring the red highlights it brought out in her still baby-fine hair. "Now, you scrub all the dirt off the potatoes," I'd said. "And then we will bake them." "Okay," she said. And then, "Mommy? Did the mother come yet?" It took me a moment to remember what she was talking about. But then I kissed the top of her head and said, "Yes, she did. She's putting the egg to bed now." "How do you know?" Hannah asked, and I took a breath in, and then, with all the nonchalant authority I could muster, I said, "Well, because it's *sunset,* silly." "Oh," she said, and began scrubbing the potato, which was twice the length of her hand. It must have felt heavy for her to hold but she scrubbed it uncomplainingly.

I saw Hannah as made of bamboo, light in the wind. She was still just a child, unformed and questioning, guileless and gullible, her psyche wet clay. She was taking in what was around her and it would help make her what she would be. I realized what I needed to do. I would stay here until Hannah fell asleep, and then I would tell my mother that I wanted her out of here. That I knew who she was. That I knew everything.

AFTER I HEARD THE DEEP AND REGULAR SOUNDS of Hannah breathing, I crawled into bed beside Pete. "Are you awake?" I whispered.

"Yeah. How's Hannah?" He didn't open his eyes, but he turned onto his side, facing me.

"She feels terrible, but she finally fell asleep. Pete, tomorrow I'm telling my mother she has to leave."

Now his eyes opened. "Laura—"

"She ruined one of her own children. She's not going to ruin ours."

"She didn't ruin Hannah. She said something at the time that—"

"She's diabolical, Pete!"

"Shhhhhhhh!" He turned on the light.

"I don't care if she hears!" But I did lower my voice to say, "Why do you defend her? Why are you so easy on her when you know what she did to my sister?"

"I *don't* know everything that happened between your sister and your mother. I don't know yet! And neither do you. We might never know."

"Well, I know this. If she can make a kid who already feels terrible feel worse, if she can *on purpose* do such a thing, she's capable of more."

"But Laura, think of what else she's done. Think of how the kids feel about her, how Hannah loves her!"

"So did Caroline, Pete. Caroline adored her. Until she woke up. I'm telling you, I am throwing her out. She cannot be around my children."

"Maybe you need to just . . . sleep on it."

"Nothing will change my mind, Pete. If you don't want to see, don't see. But nothing will change my mind."

"Laura, if Hannah can forgive your mother for overreacting one time, can't you?"

"Hannah forgives her because she doesn't know what's coming next."

"Neither do you! Laura, people make mistakes, sometimes they make terrible mistakes. Forgive us our trespasses, you know?"

"Yeah, right. Directed at Our Father, who art in heaven. On earth is not like heaven."

He was quiet for a moment, and then he said, "Well, here's what I believe. Sometimes it is. I guess it's up to us to try to make it so. At any rate, at least make sure your mother was the one at fault before you blame her entirely for the way Caroline is."

*"How?"* But then I knew how. I would do what Caroline had been asking me to do. I would sit with the two of them while Caroline opened that big black bag.

*It is by itself, barely adhering to the center of the page with Scotch tape turned butterscotch yellow and brittle to the touch. The photo is small in size and the image is blurred, evidence of the imperfect skills of the photographer. But there is a loveliness about it, a kind of peace. In the center is a large tree, leaves in the barely budding phase. There are a few high clouds in the sky, the cirrus variety that look like stretched cotton candy. There is an oblique slant to them; they look as though a giant hand has brushed over them, urging them ever upward. The land is empty-looking; in early spring, not much would have been growing yet. But there are low hills in the background, and a far-off line of evergreens lends the picture a softness, a kind of promise. Beneath the picture, in labored child's writing, is this: BY: CAROLINE.*

*THIS IS NUMBER ONE! There are no more.*

# 23

IN THE MORNING, I DRESSED AND CAME INTO THE kitchen to find Pete at the table, eating breakfast. "I'm going to call Jim Pearson," he said.

"Why don't we just go over there? He'll be up—he's an early riser."

"Okay. All right." He got up, shoved his hands in his pockets, cleared his throat. "Ready?"

Together we crossed the street to go to the Pearsons' door. I rang the bell, then looked over at Pete. I was as nervous as he. Anything could happen. A lawsuit.

The door opened, and Jim said, "Oh, hey, I was just going to call you two. Come on in."

We entered the hallway and followed Jim into the living room. "Have a seat," he told us, and we moved to the sofa, sitting close to each other. On the floor, I saw a pile of books I remembered reading to Hannah when she was a little girl; she must have brought them over. I looked away from them.

"I just want you to know we're so sorry about what happened," Pete said. "How is Nicki?"

"She's *fine*. She'll have a tiny little scar that will all but disappear when she gets older. She's being released this morning. I'm getting ready to go and get her and my wife. How about Hannah? Is she okay?"

I had an impulse to turn triumphantly to Pete and say, *See?* Instead, I said, "She feels pretty terrible."

"I was afraid of that," Jim said. "When I was in fifth grade, I accidentally hit a kid in the head with a baseball bat. It ended up that he was all right, but man! I had some sleepless nights." He reached into his pocket and pulled out his billfold. "I never paid her."

"It's all right," I said, and felt Pete lightly touch my arm. He thought I should take it for her.

"I'd like her to have it," Jim said. "And I'd like you to tell her that almost the first thing Nicki said when I saw her is that she'd like to have Hannah sit again. Up until the time of the accident, they were having a great time. Hannah helped Nicki make a coat for her doll, and she and Tyler made a picture using popcorn kernels. He's got it on his wall."

"I'll tell her," I said.

"If we don't call her right away, it's because we do have a regular sitter—"

"I understand."

Pete rose and offered his hand to Jim. "I know you must be eager to go. Thanks so much for understanding. I really appreciate it."

"It's fine, Pete. Let's go out for a beer soon."

When we walked back home, I said, "That's the kind of compassion I would have hoped for from my mother."

"He's had a day to get used to it, Laura. And he had a doctor tell him his daughter was going to be fine. He didn't see her standing there screaming with blood all over her."

I said nothing until we arrived home. When we came into the kitchen, my mother was at the stove, fussing with something in a frying pan. "I'm serving Hannah breakfast in bed," she said.

Pete looked at me. "I'm going to the store and catch up on some paperwork," he said. Meaning, *It's all yours.*

I sat at the table, watching my mother. It was still familiar to me, the movement of her back in a robe, fixing breakfast at a stove. I knew precisely how high she would hold the spatula, how briskly she would scramble the eggs. "Hannah's up already?" I asked.

"She is. I heard her calling for you, and I—"

"I'll be right back." I went up into Hannah's room and found her leaning back against her pillows, reading a book.

"Hey." I sat beside her.

She marked her place, put the book down. "Where were you?"

"Dad and I went to talk to Mr. Pearson." Her expression changed, and I said, "Don't worry, he's fine. And Nicki's fine too—she's coming home today, and she'll have a very, very small scar that will end up disappearing completely. And you know what she wants?"

"What?" She wouldn't look at me.

"She wants you to babysit again. She really liked you. And Mr. Pearson did too. He sent over the money you earned."

She looked up, her eyes full of tears. "I don't want it. And I don't ever want to babysit again."

"Oh, Hannah. I know how bad you feel, honey. I really do. But if you never babysit again, you'll deprive a lot of kids of some really wonderful experiences. It was an accident. Nobody blames you. In fact, Jim told us about a kid he once hit accidentally with a baseball bat!"

Half a smile. "Really?"

"Yes!"

"Was he okay?"

"Yes! He was!"

"Well, I think I'll wait awhile. But I'll tell Mr. and Mrs. Pearson I'm sorry. I'll write them a note."

"Okay." I kissed her forehead. "So you're having breakfast in bed, are you?"

"Yeah, I woke Grandma up but she was really nice. She said she'd make me breakfast. And she said she was sorry for yelling at me."

"Did she? Well, I'm glad she did." I waited for a moment, then said, "Hannah? I'm going to take Grandma home today."

"You are?"

"Uh-huh. I think I'll drive her back."

"Does she want to go home?"

I stood and straightened Hannah's covers. "Yeah, I think she's probably ready to go back. It's hard to be away from home for too long. You know."

"But . . . she said she wished she could live here."

"When? When did she say that?"

Hannah tilted her head, looked deeply into my eyes. "Are you *mad*?"

"No! When did she say that?"

Hannah shrugged. "A lot of times. To me, and to Anthony too. Didn't she tell you?"

"Here we are," my mother said, and walked into the room with a tray. Hannah and I exchanged glances, and I said, "You go ahead and eat, honey. I'll talk to you later." Then to my mother, "Mom? Can we go downstairs and talk for a minute?"

"Wait!" Hannah said.

I turned around, and Hannah said to my mother, "Could I . . . I need to talk to my mom alone, Grandma. Okay?"

"That's fine," my mother said lightly. "My goodness, I don't mind. A person has to have privacy sometimes. You enjoy your breakfast."

She closed the door in as pointed a way as it was possible to do. I sat down again, at the foot of Hannah's bed.

"Don't make her leave, Mom."

"It's time for her to go home."

"*Why?*"

"Hannah, I can't explain everything right now. But"—I lowered my voice—"there are some things I need to find out. I don't feel I can really trust her. She's capable of bad things. I think she—"

Hannah dropped her fork and covered her ears. "She's my *grandma*!"

I wanted to say, *Yes, and you are my daughter.* Instead, I uncovered her ears and said, "Okay. Okay. Don't worry. Eat your breakfast, okay? Don't worry."

Downstairs, my mother sat at the kitchen table with a toasted English muffin covered with her usual slathering of butter. She loved butter, and she used to put it on my sandwiches when she made my school lunches. I would tell her every day not to, and the next day she would put it on again, because that was the way she liked *her* sandwiches. She had just begun to take a bite, but when she saw me she stopped and put the muffin back on her plate.

"Eat," I said, and surprised myself by the nasty tone of my voice. I moved to sit across from her, reached out to touch her hand. "I'm sorry. I didn't mean that the way it sounded. I just meant, don't stop eating on my account."

She said nothing. I could see her heart beating in her throat, saw sleep in the corner of one of her eyes, something I was sure I'd never seen before. I didn't know if my mother was becoming less meticulous or simply couldn't see well anymore. Whatever the reason, I could feel my resolve weakening. Should I really ask her to leave my house, insist that she do so, when everyone else in the family seemed so much against it, or at least deeply ambivalent? Was I making too much out of what she said to Hannah because it was the only way I could think of to support my sister? Was I now going to start cataloging my own slights, punishing my mother for putting butter on sandwiches forty years ago?

My mother is the one who took us kids out one hot summer afternoon to pick up pizza at a parlor where the temperature was truly unbearable. It wasn't the temperature outside or the blasting ovens on the inside; the air-conditioning had gone out in the place. The woman who waited on us had sweat pouring off her; yet she smiled pleasantly and wished us a happy picnic—we were going to a park across the street. After we ate lunch, my mother took us into the florist next to the pizza parlor, bought the woman a lovely bouquet, and then asked me to give it to her. "But what should I tell her?" I asked my mother, a little angry that she wouldn't deliver it herself. "You don't have to tell her anything," my mother said. "She'll know we just appreciate her being so pleasant under the circumstances." I think she wanted me to do it so I could enjoy the reaction, so I could see it was possible to bring joy to a stranger and take away more for yourself.

And once, when I whimsically suggested that I wanted my teddy bears to get married, my mother immediately manufactured a wedding between two stuffed animals. She made a paper-towel runner in the upstairs hall, put a white cake in the oven, and, while it baked, ran to a nearby party store for supplies. She bought napkins with a wedding motif, and silver and white crepe paper, and a plastic bride and groom to put atop the cake. She made Steve, then eight, be the minister; she made me the matron of honor, and she made herself the "guests." Caroline was supposed to be the soloist, but at the last minute she refused to sing. "There's no music," she said petulantly, and she sat off to the side, watching the ridiculous but tender ceremony and picking at one of her toes. You could look up her faded red shorts and see her underwear, which to my mind ruined the ceremony entirely.

But. There was also everything Caroline had told me. There were the brief flashes of memory and understanding that I was beginning to have. If one's life was about anything, it was about making choices, taking risks, deciding what was worthwhile and what was not. I could not have my mother with my children when so much was still in doubt.

My mother pushed her plate away and sat up straighter. "What do you want to talk about, Laura?"

"This is hard for me to say, Mom, so bear with me. But things are kind of . . . well, I need a little time to be alone with my family. I think it might be best if I drive you home."

"When?"

"Today."

She drew in a sharp breath, started to say something, and then rose abruptly to carry her dishes to the sink. "You can take me to the airport right now." She turned on the water hard to rinse out her cup and ended up splattering herself. She jumped back and dropped the cup, shattering it, then put her hands to her face and began to weep. I walked slowly over to her, stepped past the shards of china, and put my arms around her. She hugged me back abruptly, tightly, and then whispered into my ear, "You know, don't you?"

I nodded. "Yes."

"Caroline told you everything?"

"Yes. And I know it was you who came after Caroline with the knife that day, Mom."

Inside myself, a frayed string on which hung a last hope: *Say no. Say you never did that, it never happened.* But what she said was, "Yes."

I closed my eyes, swallowed. "And . . . I know about Claire. Aunt Fran told me."

She stepped away from me, sighed deeply. There passed a long moment during which she would not look at me. Then she said, "I'll go and pack. And then I would like to be driven to the airport."

I wanted to say, You know what? Your days of dictating are over. Your needs coming first? That's over. But all I said was, "I'm going to pack too, Mom. I'll drive you home."

IT TOOK TWO HOURS OF DRIVING before either of us said anything. While my mother packed, I rather abruptly told my children what I was going to do, then called Pete at the store to tell him the same. When we left, I looked away when my mother hugged Anthony and Hannah and tried not to mind their stiffness when I hugged them too. When I spoke privately to Anthony, telling him I was taking Grandma home because I wasn't comfortable with her behavior during the babysitting incident, he said, "God, Mom, you're pretty hard on people." I wanted to argue my case, but I remembered Hannah's reaction when I tried to tell her more. In the end, I just told him I'd see him in a few days and left. At the right time, I hoped I'd find the words.

It was odd, having my mother beside me in front. I couldn't remember a time when I drove her for any length of time. It didn't compute, somehow, to see her knee in my peripheral vision, to feel the small moves she made adjusting herself on the seat.

I was still full of such a mix of conflicting emotions. Not the least of these was still a kind of anger at Caroline, for bringing all this on. I recognized it was unfair, this lack of love and support one should have for a sister. But I didn't have it. We grew up virtual strangers to each other. It was hard, at this age, to try to create a natural bond I never had, to feel for someone who so often made me impatient. If I were to meet Caroline as someone other than my sister, could I feel sympathy for her? If what she was saying was true, I could. And it was true.

So here beside me, in the form of my mother, was the woman who did all those terrible things to her child. How did one begin a dialogue with such a person? Especially when she was such a different mother to Steve and me. Did she deserve a last chance to defend herself? Did the fact that she was such a recent widow entitle her to more consideration? Should I begin by telling her that things would be different between us from now on, I wondered, and that for one thing she would not be left alone with my children? Or should I not worry about it at the moment and instead start figuring out how I was going to get her and Caroline and me together, thus putting Caroline's concerns first? Wasn't it time Caroline came first?

I turned off the radio. "Mom?"

"Don't let's talk now," she said. "Let me just get home first." I thought I understood her need for the anchoring influence of one's own things.

"Okay. But I want to tell you, we're going to meet with Caroline as soon as we get there, you and I. It's something she asked for, and we're going to give it to her."

"All right."

I was shocked. I had expected anything but matter-of-fact cooperation. I snuck a look over at her: a faded beauty. A woman staring straight ahead seeing nothing. A woman whose hands were in her lap, fists clenched, waiting out the miles.

I turned on the radio again. Then I said, "I'm going to stop for gas soon. I'll get us some sandwiches."

"All right."

"And I'm going to call Caroline to say we're on the way."

"Yes, I know. I know you will." Her hand to her earlobe, checking for the diamond there. Her only ally on this her judgment day.

# 24

I ONCE WENT TO A PHOTO EXHIBIT AT A MUSEUM OF
modern art. Included in it was a display of school photos
taken in the early sixties, children mostly around the age
of eleven who had been hauled out of class to line up and
then sit on a chair before a school photographer, one of
those skinny men with bad breath and a defeated attitude
who ask kids over and over to smile without caring, particularly, if they smile or not. The pictures at the museum
were framed, and there were yards of foil silver stars on
wire wrapped around them and pinned up on the wall between them. There were tiny white lights everywhere,
too, the kind you put on Christmas trees. Otherwise, the
room was dark and the walls were painted black. I remember thinking that this worked well to contribute to the
mood of going back in time, of feeling encapsulated. You
felt yourself disappearing before all these photos of kids
you didn't know, yet did.

Most of the photos were funny, the kind of thing you point to and giggle: the goofy expressions, the cowlicks, the braces, the glasses, the collars with one side up and one side down. But there was one photo that stopped me in my tracks, that had me standing unsmiling before it for a long time. After I left the exhibit to go and look at other things, I went back to stand before that photo again. Then, as I was putting my coat on, getting ready to go home, I went to go and look at it for a third time. It was a little girl, straight-mouthed and clear-eyed. There was something so compelling in her expression, so deep in her eyes. Looking at her photo had a kind of pulling effect: Standing still, I felt as though I moved into her, then felt inside my own chest the weight of her great sorrow.

I know now—knew then too, probably—that that photo was Caroline to me. And now, years away from what happened to her and what I contributed to, I was ready to move forward in a way that might make a real difference. I felt a little—a *little*—like I did the time I signed up for tap-dancing lessons at age forty-seven. Not that I saw my intentions as trivial. It was just that I was so late, and I had so much doubt about my abilities.

ABOUT TEN MINUTES FROM CAROLINE'S HOUSE, my mother began to speak. "I read once about how anxiety on behalf of a child can trans- form itself into aggression against a child."

I said nothing, but what I was thinking was, *I read once about how the weakest of a litter is sometimes destroyed by its siblings. We are all guilty.*

She said, "I don't mean this as an excuse. But I was so broken- hearted after the baby died! I felt her every minute of every day for so long. Reaching for me. I couldn't climb out of this terrible despair. Aunt Fran used to come and take you, and I would just sit in the rocking chair in Claire's bedroom and cry and cry and cry. I don't think I knew my own mind for a long time. Then, after Caroline was born, I told your father I thought I was going crazy. I told him I didn't love her, that sometimes I felt I hated her, and he said, No, no, you're fine, you've just had a shock, you'll be fine, of course you love your baby, everybody can see that. And then Caroline was so difficult from the very beginning, such a dark child, so oversensitive and demanding, really, you might not realize this, but she was very demanding. Maybe I had Steve in part to prove to myself that I wasn't a monster. Maybe—"

"Mom. I think Caroline needs to hear this too. Let's wait till we get there." Somewhere, a pinprick of sympathy for her. A memory of her lifting me up, pointing at something she wanted me to see, kissing my cheek, and then gently wiping away the marks of her red lipstick. A memory of her deteriorating handwriting on the tags of the gifts she sent for my last birthday. Finally, oddly, perhaps, a memory of a scene in a movie about Mary Kay, of Mary Kay Cosmetics, where she is sitting on her bed as an old woman, wigless and without makeup, putting blusher on her rapt young granddaughter, telling her in a soft voice why it's "*verrrry* important to put it on your chin and forehead as well as your cheeks. Right?" Her old bones and sunken chest. The tenets on which she built her life now outdated and irrelevant, almost foolish. Though not to her granddaughter. Her granddaughter had her own way of seeing her, and her own relationship to her.

I have a friend from college—Anne—who was recently cleaning out her daughter's room after her daughter left home to move to her first apartment. I'd always thought they had a terrific relationship, and I told Anne that day how much I admired it. But she said, "You know, I was moving some books off my daughter's shelf and I was looking at all the titles and it was such a wonderful mix of literature: novels in French, texts on physics and Dutch art, poetry by Neruda, and then—the killer—*My Goodnight Book*." This was a picture book Anne used to read to her daughter over and over when she was a little girl. She'd had no idea her daughter had kept it. She started bawling, not only because of the engulfing nostalgia but because she had no idea her daughter had read those *other* books; they'd never talked about a single one. "I always vowed that I would really know my children—and they me," she said. "You just can't do all you intend. Every mother fails."

I felt the quick sting of tears; one rolled down my cheek. Out of the corner of my eye, I saw my mother handing something over to me. A folded handkerchief, a floral one, lace around the edges, perfumed. "You might need this yourself," I said, not looking at her.

"I have another," she said. "I'm never without them. Don't you know that?"

WHEN WE KNOCKED ON CAROLINE'S DOOR, I was prepared for anything. I accepted that she might carry on for hours, or refuse to talk, or have white bandages wrapped around her wrists that she waved accusingly in front of us. She was completely unreadable when I called and told her we were coming, when I told her about Claire, when I told her that Mom knew I knew everything.

The door opened. Caroline was wearing black pants and a red top, no makeup. She had her hair pulled back, some small hoop earrings on. There were dark circles under her eyes, but her face was blank, noncommittal. From inside, I smelled something chocolaty.

"Come in," she said, and stepped aside while we went down the hall and into the living room. When we were all seated, Caroline said, "I needed to tell, Mom."

My mother nodded. She had not yet looked at Caroline.

"It would have been worse to not tell."

Silence.

It went on and on. I thought of Pete and the kids. I wondered what the dog outside was barking at. I thought of all that might happen after this encounter, wondered whether Caroline would finally free herself from all of us, for which I certainly would not blame her. I wondered how many years it would take for this to settle.

Finally, my mother spoke, her voice low and tentative. "Caroline? Can you tell me about a time in your childhood when you were happy? One time?"

I sat up straighter, ready to hear the onslaught my mother deserved. The selfishness! The cruelty—again! To focus on what was not even the point of this meeting, to make a wounded person turn away from her own vital needs to take care of you!

My sister quietly cleared her throat. "There was a time shortly after . . . It was that summer, a few days before Steve and Laura were going to come home from camp. You and I went for a walk. We were going to buy some groceries, I think. But on the walk, you told me about when you had to get glasses, and Aunt Fran didn't, and how mad you were. And how ugly the glasses you got were. You said they were so heavy and black, you used to hide them all the time, and one time Grandma sat on them because you hid them under a sofa cushion, and she sat on them and broke them and she was really angry. You hid from her for hours in the lilac bushes and Aunt Fran brought you sandwiches, though you didn't deserve them, you said, you didn't deserve them at all. You laughed and you looked so pretty; you were wearing a sky-blue skirt and a white blouse. And then you looked at me and took my hand, and you held it all the way to the store and you tried very hard not to let me see that you were crying. I remember that."

My mother sat still as a painting; it was hard to see her breathing. Then she said, "And . . . if you could please tell me what you would like me to do now. What I should do."

"Well, I made some brownies," Caroline said. "I thought we

could all have some, and then maybe we could go shopping to-gether." I looked over at her, incredulous. That's *it?* But when she looked back at me, something in the clarity of her gaze made me feel as though I understood. The conversation I had just witnessed was between the two of them and had nothing to do with me or my ex-pectations of how things should go. Also, it had nothing to do with bitterness or blame or retribution. This was what my sister was say-ing: Start here.

# 25

NEXT TO MY BED, I USED TO KEEP A PHOTOGRAPH OF
two little girls I didn't know—sisters, judging from the
way they closely resembled each other. They were sitting
on a porch swing, laughing. They were barefoot, and they
wore baggy shorts and sleeveless T-shirts; they had soda-
pop mustaches. Their foreheads were nearly touching and
their hands were moving toward each other. It was a
movement signifying love and ease, as well as a certain
sense of belonging. I kept it there because I liked looking
at it; for me, it signified the way families ought to be. People who saw it always said, "Oh, this is you and your sister." And I always laughed and said, "No, I have no *idea*
who that is." This begged another question, of course,
about why I would keep a photo of strangers next to my
bed, which was never asked and so never answered.

But Hannah, who just started sixth grade, was recently
told to write an essay defining what *family* meant. She

described this assignment, uncharacteristically, as impossible. When I asked her why, she said, "Because it's too slippery to say what a family is. It always changes." But she did write the assignment, and in it she said what I thought was a wise thing. She said that you are born into your family and your family is born into you. No returns. No exchanges.

It was reading Hannah's words that prompted me to replace the photo of the little girls I never knew with something else.

*It is winter, and Caroline and I are lying outside on the ground, making snow angels. We are head to head, and the photo was snapped when our arms were stretched up, our fingers touching. Our eyes are closed, and we are smiling.*

*I remember how carefully we stepped away from our imprints, how very much we wanted to leave behind a flawless image. And I remember standing beside her after we got up and seeing that we had done it: There in the snow before us were two perfect angels. But more snow was on the way; already tiny flakes were beginning to swirl around us. All the evidence of our little success would vanish.*

*Caroline looked up at the gathering clouds, heavy and gray, and shrugged. She said, "We can make another one. We have a lot of days left to go."*

## ABOUT THE AUTHOR

ELIZABETH BERG is the author of twelve previous novels, including the *New York Times* bestsellers *Say When, True to Form, Never Change,* and *Open House,* which was an Oprah's Book Club Selection in 2000. *Durable Goods* and *Joy School* were selected as ALA Best Books of the Year, and *Talk Before Sleep* was short-listed for the ABBY Award in 1996. The winner of the 1997 New England Booksellers Award for her body of work, she is also the author of a nonfiction work, *Escaping into the Open: The Art of Writing True.* She lives in Chicago.

ABOUT THE TYPE

This book is set in Fournier, a typeface named for Pierre Simon Fournier, the youngest son of a French printing family. He started out engraving woodblocks and large capitals, then moved on to fonts of type. In 1736 he began his own foundry and made several important contributions in the field of type design; he is said to have cut 147 alphabets of his own creation. Fournier is probably best remembered as the designer of St. Augustine Ordinaire, a face that served as the model for Monotype's Fournier, which was released in 1925.